Jessica had been acting strangely from the moment he'd answered the door that morning, and Dylan couldn't quite figure out why.

Was it because of the way things had ended between them the day before? Maybe, he thought. But then he remembered the way things had crackled between them when he'd saved her from falling. The way his body had reacted to her body's proximity, and the shame he'd felt when she'd pulled away.

She was pregnant, for crying out loud. There was no circumstance in which that didn't make her off-limits. He needed to remember that, he thought, when his heart stuttered as his eyes rested on her.

But damn it, there was just *something* about her that pulled him in. That made rational thought not matter, and made hope flare when it shouldn't. And it had nothing to do with her relationship with his sister.

He told himself to pull back, to control himself, and went over to talk with her.

Dear Reader,

Jess and Dylan's story started because I loved the idea of the billionaire next door. I'm probably not the only one, though I am fortunate enough to be in a career where I can give this fantasy the effort it deserves. Naturally, it would be in some form of romance, so this story is exactly how I imagine things would play out if I was living next door to a billionaire...

Okay, maybe not *exactly*. I doubt that I would have been best friends with said billionaire's sister, nor would I have been connected to him in any way through the baby I was carrying. So perhaps it's for the best that—for me at least—billionaires next door only exist on paper!

I hope that you enjoy Jess and Dylan's story. It's about family and friendship, about love and loyalty, and will hopefully remind you of all the wonderful relationships you have in your life. Writing their story definitely has for me, including the relationship I have with my readers: you all mean so much to me!

If you'd like to say hi, you can find me on Twitter (@theresebeharrie), Facebook (Therese Beharrie, Author) and my website (theresebeharrie.com).

I'm so happy to share *Tempted by the Billionaire Next Door* with you!

Happy reading!

Love,

Therese

Tempted by the Billionaire Next Door

—

Therese Beharrie

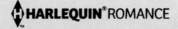

HARLEQUIN® ROMANCE

Recycling programs
for this product may
not exist in your area.

ISBN-13: 978-1-335-13513-1

Tempted by the Billionaire Next Door

First North American publication 2018

Copyright © 2018 by Therese Beharrie

Printed in U.S.A.

Therese Beharrie has always been thrilled by romance. Her love of reading established this, and now she gets to write happy-ever-afters for a living, and about all things romance in her blog at theresebeharrie.com. She married a man who constantly exceeds her romantic expectations and is an infinite source of inspiration for her romantic heroes. She lives in Cape Town, South Africa, and is still amazed that her dream of being a romance author is a reality.

Books by Therese Beharrie

Harlequin Romance

Conveniently Wed, Royally Bound

United by Their Royal Baby
Falling for His Convenient Queen

The Tycoon's Reluctant Cinderella
A Marriage Worth Saving
The Millionaire's Redemption

Visit the Author Profile page at Harlequin.com.

For Grant, my best friend.

And Jenny, for taking the squirming, questing and searching journey of friendship with me. I can't imagine doing this without you.

Praise for
Therese Beharrie

"I really enjoyed this book. It had a gutsy, sympathetic heroine, a moody hero, and the South African setting was vividly drawn. A great debut novel. I'll definitely be reading this author again."

—*Goodreads* on *The Tycoon's Reluctant Cinderella*

CHAPTER ONE

JESSICA STEYN HADN'T deliberately sought out the half-naked man who'd entertained her over the last week. But she couldn't deny that watching him had fast become her new favourite hobby.

She watched as he bent over to pick up another stack of logs—watched as the muscles of his naked back rippled, the lightest sheen of sweat defining them even more—and conceded that it was *definitely* top-notch entertainment.

Guilt poked at her, but she ignored it. It wasn't *her* fault that he wasn't wearing a shirt. Nor was it her fault that he'd made a routine of cutting up the trees in his yard. Every day at noon he emerged from the house—wearing an old T-shirt that inevitably got tossed aside about five minutes into his task—and hacked the trunks he'd cut down the day before into logs. He then placed them in a pile, before carrying them over to an enclosed area where he'd set them down and start all over again.

So, ever since she'd noticed there *was* a routine, every day at noon she would settle in front of the window that overlooked his property to enjoy the show.

Thank goodness she'd discovered him, she thought as he gulped down a bottle of water. Water that dribbled over his chin, creating an enticing path down the column of his throat, between his pecs and the impressive ridges of his abs. Her heart rate immediately skyrocketed, and she thought that maybe *she* needed a glass of water, too.

He was a pretty decent distraction in an otherwise boring day. Now that her friend and boss, Anja, was away with her husband, Chet, on business, Jess's days were mostly free. Apart from watching Mr Sexy-Next-Door.

And, of course, thinking about the child she carried.

Before her mind could take that detour—about how this child made Jess feel as if her life was actually worth something for the first time—she thought about how annoyed she was with Anja for not telling her that there *was* a Mr Sexy-Next-Door.

She'd been helping Anja manage her yoga studio for almost two years now, and this was the first time Jess had seen him. Though, to be fair, it was also the first time Jess had stayed at Anja's house for longer than a few days. But she still expected Anja to tell her about the man. Perhaps not as her boss, but as her friend.

And definitely as her *best* friend.

But all thoughts of that vanished when the top log of the stack Mr Sexy had set down started to roll. He'd already turned away, so didn't see the snowball effect of that one log. Jess pushed out of her chair, a wordless cry of warning on her lips, but it was too late. The logs had rolled under his feet and she watched in horror as he fell to the ground, twisting his body so that he landed on his hip.

Before she knew it, she was out of the front door. She had to turn back when she realised she hadn't locked the house and, after she did, she ran as fast as her swollen body would allow to her temporary neighbour's house. She said a silent prayer of thanks when she found his gate open and then she was kneeling beside him, her hands running over the chest she'd admired only minutes before.

She ignored how the grooves of his muscles, his abs, felt beneath her hands and focused on identifying whether anything was broken. She realised that he'd turned over onto his back then, but it only made her pause for a second. Then her hands were on his ankles, his calves, but, before she could feel his thighs or hips, two large hands gripped her wrists.

'I'm not opposed to having a beautiful woman run her hands over me, but maybe we should leave that particular area for when we know each other better.'

Jess felt her face burn and quickly pulled back. But her balance was off and she landed on her butt. Her hand immediately went to her stomach, but she dropped it just as quickly. Not because his eyes had followed the gesture, and the way the interest there had cooled reminded her of the dismissive looks her parents had used to give her, but because she was fairly certain the baby was fine. She hadn't fallen very hard. Though she really had to remember that pregnancy had made her clumsy.

'I'm assuming that response means you didn't knock your head on the way down.' She debated not saying anything else, but she knew she would worry if she didn't ask. 'Are you okay?'

'Yeah, I guess so. Well, as okay as you can be when someone witnesses a couple of logs trip you.' He moved to push up to his forearms, but she crawled forward and set a hand on his chest, pushing him back down.

'You should stay still until we're sure you're really fine.'

'I *am* sure. I'm fine.'

Realising he was the stubborn sort, Jess pressed a hand against his hip and nodded when he winced. 'You're not fine. I'm calling an ambulance.'

Before she could move to her feet, he grabbed her wrist again. This time, she felt the heat of his hand on her arm. Felt the callused bumps at the base of his fingers rub against her skin. She wasn't sure why it sent a flush through her body, but she stilled and then gently pulled her arm out of his grip.

His expression didn't change, though something in his eyes flickered. 'I really am fine. I'll probably have a bruise on my hip tomorrow— and my ego will probably need to be resuscitated since it was murdered so cruelly—but I promise you, I'm fine.'

He sat up then, and she let him. 'Besides,' he continued with a smile that made the flush in her body go hotter, 'if I'm not fine, maybe you'll come to my rescue again.'

'Unlikely,' she replied, ignoring the way her lips wanted to curve at his words. 'I just happened to be looking out of my window when you fell.'

It sounded legitimate, she thought, and almost patted herself on the back when she saw he'd bought her excuse. Good thing, too. She wasn't sure how she could explain the real reason she'd seen him.

'I appreciate you wanting to help me. Are you a doctor?'

'No.'

'Nurse?'

She shook her head.

'So, you just ran over when you saw me fall without any medical skills whatsoever?'

'I was a lifeguard when I was a teenager.' A choice her parents had disapproved of heartily. Funny how they'd chosen to be interested in something so insignificant when they'd ignored everything else in her life. When they'd ignored *her*. 'I have first-aid experience, and falls were the first thing they taught us to deal with.'

'I stand corrected.' His smile was more genuine now, less cocky, and yet it had the same effect on her body.

Or maybe it was the fact that he still didn't have a shirt on, and she was being treated to her afternoon entertainment close-up.

She almost lifted a hand to check whether she was drooling.

'Well, now that I know you're okay I should probably be off.' She took a long time to get to her feet, and cursed silently when she saw how smoothly he did it.

'How can I repay you?'

She snorted. 'For what? Rushing over here and embarrassing us both?'

'Why would you be embarrassed?'

Good question. 'Because clearly you were fine and I panicked over nothing?'

'You panicked?'

She rolled her eyes. 'It was a hard fall, okay? I was worried.'

She couldn't tell what had changed on his face, but something had. And it made his already too perfect features seem even more appealing. 'So, I'm repaying you for being worried. It's not often that people care.'

'No, it isn't,' she agreed, feeling the words hit a little too close to home. 'But I don't need to be repaid. You're fine. Right?' He nodded. 'So, I'll be seeing you.'

She turned to leave and managed to get a few steps away from the gate before his voice called out, 'Which window?'

She turned back. 'What?'

'From which window did you see me fall?'

'That one.' She nodded to the window on the second level of the house next door, grateful that the chair she'd been sitting on—or the chips she'd been eating while watching him—wasn't visible.

'That's my sister's house.'

It took a moment for her mind to process the

new information. 'Your sister?' she repeated. *'You're* Dylan?'

'Yeah,' he said, his forehead creasing. 'Who are you? And why are you staying in my sister's house?'

'I'm Jess. Jessica,' she added quickly. 'I'm staying at the house while Anja and Chet are away.'

His features tightened. 'Away where?'

'Sydney. They wanted to get Anja's new yoga studio up and running before the—' She caught herself before it was too late. She couldn't tell Dylan about the baby. Anja would kill her. And she didn't need to upset one of the few people who cared about her. 'Does she know you're here?'

'No.'

'Oh.'

There was a long stretch of silence before either of them spoke again. And then she asked, 'You've been back for at least a week. Why haven't you come over? Or tried to call her?'

He frowned. 'How do you know how long I've been back for?'

Jess felt her eyes widen, her cheeks heat, before she managed to reply with something other than *I've been watching you.* 'I heard the garbage truck pick up your bin earlier this week.' She held her breath and hoped he'd buy the somewhat lame excuse.

'And how do you know that I haven't tried to call her?'

'She…would have told me.'

He studied her. 'How exactly do you know Anja?'

Something about the way he asked it put her back up. 'I'm her PA.'

'She let her PA stay in her house?' There was barely a pause before he continued. 'She would tell her PA if her brother called her?'

Jess straightened. 'Yes. Your sister and I are also friends. Good friends.' She kept her hand from going to her stomach—to the proof of the bond that she and Anja shared—and forced herself to calm down when an inner voice questioned why she was responding so defensively. 'I didn't realise it was you when I came over.'

'But you knew I lived next door?'

'Yes,' she replied, but it got her thinking about why it hadn't occurred to her that Mr Sexy-Next-Door was actually Anja's brother. 'I knew you lived next door, but Anja didn't tell me *which* next door you lived in.'

'And you never asked?'

You're not exactly a topic of conversation either of us readily bring up. 'It didn't matter.'

'Because my sister doesn't talk about me?'

'Because you weren't here.'

Though both answers were true, it seemed as

if Dylan cared more about the option she'd offered. Because when he'd given *his* option his face hadn't tightened the way it had after *she'd* spoken. Hurt hadn't flashed across his face, quickly followed by a blankness she couldn't help but feel was desperate.

'Why *are* you here?' she said after a moment, unable to help herself.

'I live here.' There was a beat of silence. 'This is my home.'

'It hasn't been,' she reminded him, still compelled by reasons she wasn't quite sure of. 'Not for the last two years.'

'No, it has been,' Dylan replied softly. 'But even the best of us run away from home sometimes, don't we?'

Her heart stalled, reminding her of the old car she'd seen just that morning, spluttering down the road in front of Anja's house. Why did it feel as if he was talking about *her*? *To* her? As if he instinctively knew that she'd turned her back on the place she'd once called home? As if he knew that she'd run from the parents who hadn't cared enough to even try to make her believe that they wanted her to stay?

'When are they coming back?' Dylan asked gruffly. Jess shook her head, ignoring the need to push for more answers. To find out why telling her he'd run from home had clearly upset him. It was none of her business.

'The end of the month.' Though Jess had a feeling it would be a lot sooner once she told Anja that Dylan had returned. 'How long *have* you been back?'

'You were right,' he replied. 'About a week.'

So he'd been chopping up wood since the day he'd returned, she thought, and forced away the sudden disappointment that came from knowing she'd no longer be able to watch him. How could she, knowing who he was?

Older brother of her best friend. Uncle to the child she carried.

'Do you know where I've been?'

'The UK?' He nodded. 'Yeah, Anja told me you've been away for…business.'

'Clearly that isn't all she told you,' he said with a self-deprecating smile.

'No.'

The smile dimmed. 'There's a lot you seem to know about me, Jessica, and yet I haven't even heard about you.'

'Does that surprise you?'

'No.' A fleeting shadow of pain darkened his features. 'But I'm back now.'

'So you are.'

'And I'd like to have my return start on the right foot.'

Something pulsed in the air between them, but Jess refused to acknowledge it. 'Yeah, okay. Go for it.'

He smiled at her, and this time it wasn't laden with emotion. It was an easy, natural smile she imagined he'd give when he saw an old friend, or during his favourite movie. But it sent an unnatural frisson through her body.

'You should have lunch with me.'

'No,' she said immediately.

'You have somewhere else to be?'

'No, but—'

'Then have lunch with me.'

'No, thank you,' she said more firmly, hoping none of the panic she felt was evident in her voice. 'You were…busy before I interrupted.'

'After what happened, I think I'm done for the day.'

'I really don't think I should—'

'Please.' His smile widened and she almost felt faint. 'I'd like to get to know the woman staying in my sister's house. The woman who's clearly a good friend of hers.' He paused. 'That's what I meant by having my return start on the right foot. If you and I are on good terms when Anja gets back…'

The seconds ticked by, and then Jess narrowed her eyes. 'You're *schmoozing* me!'

Surprise captured his features, and then he

laughed. A loud, genuine laugh that started at
those fantastic abs and went all the way up to
his perfect hair. It was fascinating to watch. The
even angles of his face were animated with joy,
those chocolate-whisky eyes she only now noticed he shared with his sister alight with ap-
preciation.

She'd never been much of a beard woman,
but Dylan's stubble was dissuading her of that
belief. She loved that his skin reminded her of
oak—not too light, not too dark. And she *really* loved that he still didn't have a shirt on, so
she could appreciate that colour over hard, defined muscle...

'If I told you I was, would that make you want
to have lunch with me any less than you already
do?' he asked, interrupting her hormone-driven
thoughts.

'Probably.' She waited. 'So, are you?'

Now he chuckled. 'No.'

She tilted her head. Watched him. 'You're
the CEO of an international engineering company. I'd imagine that requires some measure
of intelligence.'

'You're saying I'm not intelligent?'

'Only if you expect me to believe that you're
not trying to...charm me into having lunch with
you.'

'Well, I *am* taking some time off from work.

Perhaps that's why I'm off my game. Why I've made such an unforgivable mistake.'

'You're still doing it!'

He smiled. 'I can't help it.'

'Great. It'll make my refusal so much easier then.'

'No, wait,' he said, grabbing her wrist when she turned. He let go when she turned back. Her skin prickled. 'I'm sorry. It's just…easier to schmooze than to…earnestly ask you to have lunch with me.'

'Why do you want to have lunch with me so badly?'

'You're Anja's friend and…and I'd like to show her that I'm serious about coming back to fix things. That's why I'm here,' he told her softly. 'I want to fix what I broke when I left, and if you and I are on good terms…' He shrugged. 'I wasn't lying about that, Jess.'

As Jess studied him she felt herself soften. She hated that she did, but she couldn't ignore the emotion behind his words. The hope. She also couldn't ignore how much it spoke to her own desire. The deep, dark one that she would never have admitted aloud to anyone.

That some day her parents would show up for her, just like it seemed Dylan had for Anja. That some day they'd want to fix things with her just as badly as Dylan clearly wanted to with his sister.

It was a stupid hope, one her experiences growing up had taught her not to entertain. But still, it made her want to say yes to Dylan. That, and the desire to prevent the child she carried from growing up in the tension, the broken-ness that currently existed in Anja's family. The same kind of tension and brokenness that Jess had grown up with.

Jess knew Anja was stubborn, and she wouldn't let the brother who'd left her after their father had died just come strolling back into her life. Not when that brother had broken her heart by leaving. Not when he'd broken his promise to always be there for her.

'I don't know why you left, Dylan,' Jess said softly, 'or why you didn't come home for two years. That's probably none of my business... though what I'm about to ask you falls under that category, too. But...why haven't you come over to speak with Anja since you got back?'

It was such a long time before he answered that Jess was sure he wouldn't answer her at all. 'I didn't know whether she'd want to see me, and staying away, keeping my mind and body busy with menial tasks...they were all excuses to postpone the inevitably difficult conversation I would have to have with her.'

Surprised by his candour—and more than a little touched—Jess nodded. 'Okay.'

'Okay?'

'Okay,' she repeated. She waited a beat before she said, 'You better have enough food to feed a pregnant woman, Dylan.'

It took Dylan a moment to realise what he'd done. Another to process what he'd said. And even then he wasn't sure what he was doing. Inviting a woman he barely knew into his home? Offering to make her lunch? Sharing his intention of fixing things with Anja? Hoping that she'd be able to give him some insight into his sister?

It was crazy, but his craziness was dipped in desperation. Desperation because his sister hadn't spoken to him—not properly—in almost two years. Desperation because his plan to speak with her when he got home wasn't working.

Because every time he'd wanted to go over to her house to talk with her he'd remembered her face when he'd left. He'd remembered how broken she'd looked, how her voice had cracked when she'd said goodbye.

How he'd left anyway.

And now, when he'd finally told himself he would go to see her *that night*, it turned out she wasn't even there.

He was disappointed, and perhaps that had been another reason for his invitation to Jess. But then the desperation, the craziness, the disappointment had landed him a meal with a beautiful woman, so was it really that bad?

Yes, an inner voice answered him. *Of course* it was. Because though the beautiful woman knew things about his sister that *he* didn't know—that he wanted to know—she was also pregnant. *Pregnant*. Which meant someone had got her pregnant. His eyes searched her hand for a ring, but they didn't find one.

It sent an absurd surge of hope through him, and he rolled his eyes as he led the way into his house. He bent down when he heard the scurry of paws against the wooden floor and fussed over his Labrador, Daisy, when she came bounding around the corner.

But she quickly lost interest in him and made her way to the woman he'd invited for lunch. Dylan watched as Jess's face lit up and she lowered—carefully, he saw—before rubbing his dog vigorously. It sent another surge through him, but this time it was warmth. A bubble of warmth that floated from his heart and settled in his belly.

A bubble that abruptly popped when he remembered that no wedding ring didn't mean that she was available.

And that a baby meant she *definitely* wasn't available.

'Daisy, back,' he snapped, the words coming out harsher than he'd intended because of his thoughts. The dog gave him a beseeching look but stepped back and sat, and Dylan offered a hand to help Jess up.

'Sorry about that. She gets a little excited around people.'

He sucked in his breath at the sizzle he felt coming from her hand. Held his breath when the vanilla scent she wore settled in his nose. As soon as she was steady, he broke the contact.

'Don't worry. I love dogs.'

'Do you have any?'

Sadness dulled her eyes. 'No, my parents weren't really fans of pets when I was younger. Or children.' She laughed breathlessly, but he could tell that it was meant to cover up her mistake. She hadn't meant to tell him that.

Well, that makes two of us, he thought, remembering what he'd told her about coming home. And because of it he didn't address her slip. Instead, he approached it from a different angle.

'Why don't you have any now? Doesn't your husband want pets either?'

'No husband.' She shrugged. 'I'm just your typical unwed pregnant woman, I guess.'

She didn't look too bothered by it, which forced him to ignore the hope that stirred inside him again. 'Somehow I doubt that.'

'That I'm unwed and pregnant?'

'That you're typical.'

'You barely know me, Dylan.'

Her eyes met his and it felt as if lightning flashed between them. The seconds ticked by, the current of energy between them grew more intense, but neither of them looked away. Eventually, he said, 'What are you in the mood to eat?'

A moment passed, and then he could see her force herself to relax. 'Do you have peanut butter?'

It was such a strange request that it broke the tension he still felt inside him. 'Yeah, I think so.' He narrowed his eyes. 'You want *peanut butter*? I'm pretty sure there's something more substantial in the fridge.'

'Peanut butter is plenty substantial,' she replied defensively. 'Especially if you serve it with those bananas over there.'

She nodded to the fruit bowl on his kitchen table, and he felt the smile on his face almost before he even knew it was there. 'Peanut butter and banana?'

'Peanut butter and banana,' she confirmed, and smiled. 'I tried to warn you about what you were getting into by inviting a pregnant woman for lunch.'

'Yeah, you did,' he answered, though he struggled for the words because her smile was so...*distracting*. As was her face—the smooth curves of its oval shape, the high cheekbones, those cinnamon eyes, the glossy olive of her skin, those generous lips...

Even her *hair* was distracting. The dark brown strands were clipped back into a messy style that he couldn't decide whether he liked. Mostly because it made him want to tidy it up. *No*, he corrected his thoughts immediately. Because it made him want to muss it up even *more*.

Her clothing was loose, hiding the curve of her stomach. That was why he hadn't noticed she was pregnant at first—though he'd discovered it pretty quickly, so he couldn't blame ignorance for the fact that he'd flirted with her.

But he didn't want to think about what he could blame flirting with her on, so he was glad when she spoke.

'Who looked after Daisy while you were away?'

'Actually, I got her in London and then brought her back with me.'

Daisy wagged her tail when he looked over at her and love filled his heart. She'd saved him from depression, from the loneliness of his grief and anger. From his guilt. And she'd needed him in a way that was more simple than he could ever remember being needed.

His experience of being needed by his mother and sister had always—*always*—been complicated. And he blamed himself. *He'd* been the one who'd chosen to look after their family when his father had abandoned them. When his father had decided that gambling was more important than the woman he'd married. Than his children...

Dylan had been the one to take care of the household when his father's abandonment had meant that they couldn't rely on their mother any more either. So yes, maybe after they'd found out the man had died, Dylan had wanted to leave it all behind. And yes, maybe finding out a few days before his father's funeral that his mother hadn't been the victim she'd pretended to be all those years ago had given him even more incentive to leave.

But he was back now. Because his sister hadn't lied to him, hadn't betrayed him. And it was time that he stopped acting as though she had.

'Daisy's English?' Jess asked, interrupting his thoughts. She snapped a finger and Daisy was at her side in an instant. 'I've never met an English dog before,' she said, cooing at his pet.

'I don't really think they have nationalities.'

'Really? Because Daisy gives off a distinct English vibe. Like she'd invite me for tea and scones every afternoon at three.'

He laughed. 'The English actually have their tea—' He broke off at her smirk, and the laugh turned into a smile. 'You don't care, do you?'

'Not unless I'm going to the UK, which is obviously not happening any time soon.'

'How far along are you?' he asked, and began to prepare their lunch. Since peanut butter and banana didn't seem quite as appealing to him, he decided on a chicken mayo sandwich for himself.

'Just over five months. Um, Dylan?' He glanced at her. 'I know the naked chef is a thing in the UK, but you not having a shirt on… Well, it's really distracting. Do you mind?'

CHAPTER TWO

His eyebrows rose, and then a grin curved his lips. 'I'm *distracting* you?'

'Yeah,' Jess said, and tilted her chin. 'Wouldn't you be distracted if I made your food half-naked? No, don't answer that,' she added quickly, when his grin turned naughty. 'It wasn't the right comparison.'

'Probably not, but I liked it.' He winked, and something flipped in her belly. She was fairly certain it wasn't the baby. 'I'll grab a T-shirt.'

He left the kitchen and finally air flowed easily through her lungs again. She hadn't noticed how hard it had been to breathe around him. But she knew it was a sure sign that she was digging a hole that she might not be able to get out of.

And it wasn't only because of how he made her feel. It was because Jess knew what Anja and Dylan's relationship was like. And because she knew how much he'd hurt her friend by leaving.

Anja hadn't even told Dylan that he was going to be an uncle. Or that his niece or nephew would be brought into the world by a surrogate. She hadn't told him about her miscarriage after years of fertility struggles, or how those struggles and that miscarriage had been the reason she'd decided to use a surrogate.

Or, Jess thought, about the fact that *she* was that surrogate.

Jess couldn't say she agreed with her friend's silence. But then, Jess didn't understand the dynamic between siblings since she didn't have any. Nor did she understand what it was like to be part of a real family unit, where hurt and betrayal resulted from a member of that unit doing something the others didn't approve of.

She could barely call her family a *family*, for heaven's sake, let alone a *unit*.

Anja was the closest thing Jess had to family, which was why she'd offered to be Anja and Chet's surrogate. It was also why she should have been calling Anja, telling her about Dylan's return instead of waiting for him to put a shirt on so that he could make her lunch.

Jess distracted herself by looking around. The open-plan living room and kitchen were filled with light from windows and doors that made up most of the rooms' external structure. From where she stood, she could see a sunroom where she would kill to spend a few hours in the afternoon sun, furnished in muted colours that told her Dylan had incredible style, or had hired someone who did.

The living room was just as stylish, though she wasn't a big fan of the darker finishes he'd chosen. She couldn't deny that it was striking against the cream-coloured walls and solid brick fireplace, but she preferred the warmth of the kitchen. With its light waterfall counter and space around the island, it was the type of room she'd always felt more comfortable in. Understated and tasteful. Despite the fact that she'd grown up in opulence. But more likely because of it.

Before she could go down that path, Dylan walked in wearing a blue T-shirt that did nothing to detract from his sexiness. She almost sighed when her heart did a quick tumble in her chest, and a voice in her head asked her to rethink agreeing to have lunch with him.

'Still hungry?' he asked and, despite the warning, Jess heard herself say, 'Yes, I am.'

She watched him go through the rhythms of making their lunch. Watched as he didn't so much as give her an indulgent smile as he chopped the bananas and plopped them in a bowl, adding a generous dollop of peanut butter as though he'd made the meal countless times before. He finished his sandwich almost as quickly and then offered her something to drink. Before she knew it, she was following him into the sunroom she'd admired earlier.

'You didn't have to go to all this effort,' she said when they sat.

'It wasn't really an effort.' He shrugged and took a big bite of his sandwich.

She followed by spooning banana and peanut butter together, and then lifted it to her mouth. When she'd swallowed, she looked up to see him watching her, a strange expression on his face. She wasn't sure why it made her feel flushed and, though she wanted to, she didn't think she'd be able to blame it on pregnancy hormones. It had her blurting out the first thing that came to mind.

'I quite liked the trees in your backyard before you cut them down.'

'I did, too. But their leaves were clogging the gutters and, with winter coming, I thought I'd do something about it. You know, make sure the gutters work when the rain comes and have wood for the fireplace.'

Dutifully, she said, 'The fireplace is wonderful. Your whole house is.'

His eyes scanned her face and she felt another flush of heat. 'Why don't I believe you, Jess?'

'I don't know,' she replied, and quickly ate

another spoonful of peanut butter. She regretted it immediately when she noticed he was still watching her, and tried her best to act casually. When she'd swallowed, she reached for the bottle of water he'd offered her earlier and drank greedily.

'I don't really like the décor,' he continued as though there hadn't been any pause after her answer. 'But I'd already left before it was finished, so I wasn't really involved with the decision-making. Anja was, though, since we used the same guy for both our places, and I prefer hers.'

'I thought you hadn't been back since…since you left,' she finished lamely, though his expression told her he knew she'd meant to say *since your father died.*

'No, I haven't been back, but I saw pictures of both our places. I think Anja purposely gave the designer free rein to get back at me.'

'For what?'

'For leaving.' His eyes stayed on hers. 'Though you'd know more about that than I would.'

'Anja didn't tell me about the décor at all. I think it might have been before my time.'

'I wasn't talking about the décor.'

She forced herself to hold his gaze. 'I'm not sure what you're talking about.'

'About my sister's feelings about me leaving.

You mentioned that she told you more than just the fact that I'd left for business.'

'Yes.'

'Care to share?' He gave her a smile that told her he was trying to charm her again.

'No.'

The smile faltered. 'I thought—'

'What?' she interrupted. 'That I'd tell you everything your sister told me?'

He lifted an arm. Rubbed the back of his neck. 'I thought that since you were her friend, you must know…something.'

'The fact that I'm her friend means that I wouldn't tell you what I know.' Jess set down her bowl and perched on the edge of her chair. 'You didn't ask me over because you wanted the two of us to get along for Anja's sake. You asked me over so that I could tell you something that would help *you* get along with Anja.'

'And if I tell you you're right?'

'Then I'd say that it was lovely meeting you, Dylan, and wish you all the best for your return to Cape Town on my way out.'

He set his lunch down just as she had, and when he met her gaze his expression was a plea she felt hit her right in the chest. 'You must have known that was part of the reason I asked you over.'

She considered it. 'Maybe. But—'

But I wanted to believe that you wanted to get to know me.

She nearly laughed at herself. Clearly she hadn't learnt her lesson yet. People never wanted *her*.

'It seems like you want something from me that I'm not willing to give you. So it's probably best if I just leave.'

'No, Jess, don't.'

'Why not?'

'Because… I'm sorry.' He ran a hand through his hair. 'I've handled this poorly.'

'You're apologising way too much for someone who's only just met me,' she said softly. Coolly.

'So I'll be honest instead,' he replied, his voice tight. 'I wanted to know…what I was coming back to. The extent of the damage I caused by leaving.'

'I think you already do.'

He nodded. 'It would be nice to have some more…context.'

She shook her head and rose to her feet. 'I don't have context to give you. No,' she said when he opened his mouth to protest. 'Your context should come from Anja. Or your mother.'

His face darkened. 'I suppose I'll have to wait for Anja to get back then.'

Jess frowned. 'You don't have to. Your mother lives—'

'Thank you, Jess,' he interrupted, and stood with her. 'It's been lovely meeting you.'

Though Jess didn't understand his reaction, she knew that he was asking her to leave. She would have been offended if she wasn't so...curious. It was clear that Dylan had no intention of asking his mother about what had happened after he'd left. And the look on his face told her that there was a reason for that. A reason even Anja didn't know, or else Jess would know, too.

It was all very interesting, but Jess told herself it was none of her business. Again. She didn't know why she had to remind herself of that so often, so she murmured her thanks to Dylan and walked towards the door.

'Jess—' Dylan said from behind her.

'It's okay.' She opened the door and gave Daisy one last pat. 'You don't have to explain it to me. I get it.' She paused. 'It was lovely meeting you, too, Dylan. I hope your return to Cape Town is everything you hoped it would be.'

She walked out before he could reply.

Dylan stared at the door long after Jess had left, hoping that their interaction wasn't an omen for the rest of his return.

He knew the way things had spiralled between them was his fault. But he'd wanted to know what Jess knew. He told himself it was because it would give him an indication of what Anja knew. Of what his sister thought of him. But, deep down, he knew it was because he didn't want Jess to judge him based on the only thing he'd done in his life that had disappointed his sister.

Because he'd been disappointed, too, and he knew what it felt like. His entire life, his father had disappointed him. It was the best—or, rather, easiest—word to use to describe how Dylan felt about his father. About the man's gambling addiction. About his absence. And perhaps Dylan would have been able to put it all behind him after his father had died if he hadn't found out his mother had known about his father's problems before he or Anja had been born.

He and Anja had spent their entire childhood trying to comfort their mother after their father had left them. They'd no longer been children. Instead, their existence had been dedicated to keeping the woman who'd borne them from spiralling into a deep depression.

What had been the point of all that when his mother had known what she'd been getting into with his father?

When Dylan had found out, he couldn't bring himself to tell Anja. So he'd left, and tried to deal with the anger by himself, away from her.

His anger at the secret his mother had kept from them. His anger about the inexplicable grief he felt at losing a man he'd barely known.

He couldn't get past the irony that by wanting to keep Anja from the same disappointment he'd felt in their parents, *he'd* disappointed her. More than that, he thought, remembering that expression on her face when he'd told her he was leaving again. He'd *abandoned* her.

Just like his father had abandoned them.

CHAPTER THREE

JESS WOKE UP to water dripping onto her face.

It took her a moment to realise that water was dripping on to her face, and more time to realise that that wasn't a *good* thing. She sat up and looked at the ceiling, only to see a long, slim strip of water dripping across the length of the room.

Her first thought was that she needed to close the water main, and that she'd figure out where the water was coming from once she had. But when she reached down to put her shoes on, she realised that she didn't actually know where the water main was.

It took her another few minutes to figure out that she needed to ask Dylan for help, and she sighed before slipping on the soft boots she wore as slippers.

The entire floor of the passage to the front door was wet, and Jess's heart beat heavily in her chest as she walked through the water. She locked the door and then rushed to Dylan's house, and waited impatiently for him to answer after she rang the bell.

Seconds later he opened the door, and Jess found herself staring into a bare chest. Again. Why didn't he have a shirt on? she thought, annoyance straightening her spine. Didn't he realise it was *autumn*? She tilted her head up, and only then saw that his hair was mussed from sleep. Which, she discovered, had the same effect on her as his bare chest.

She forced herself to focus on the reason she'd woken him. 'Do you know where the water main to Anja's house is?'

He frowned. 'Yeah, why?'

'No time. I'll explain after you shut it off.'

His eyes swept over her, and for the first time she realised that the only thing she'd done after waking up was put her slippers on. She must look a mess, she thought, wincing internally. But she wouldn't dwell on it now. Which was probably a good thing since a voice in her head reminded her that she'd woken with water on her face, which had probably made her look even worse.

Thankfully, he seemed to take her appearance as a sign of urgency and he walked past her, barely waiting for her to waddle after him before he was at the front of Anja's house, opening a concealed hatch and reaching inside. Then he was at her side again, offering her another view of his naked chest.

'You're going to catch a cold if you don't put a shirt on,' she said, crossing her arms when her comment reminded her that she didn't have much on either. She was more dressed than he was, but her oversized shirt and black pyjama pants were not exactly the items she'd have chosen had she known she was going to see anyone, let alone *him*.

Besides, she wasn't wearing a bra, and she knew her pregnancy boobs weren't going to politely refuse to be noticed, especially in the cold.

'If you keep telling me to put a shirt on, I'm going to think you have a problem with me being shirtless. And then I'd have to ask why you have problem with me being shirtless, and I'm guessing that's not a conversation you want to have.'

As if to prove his point, he ran a hand through his hair. His biceps bulged and her throat went dry.

'I'm only worried about your health,' she managed stiffly.

'Oh, I forgot. Because of your medical background, right?' He grinned and she almost— *almost*—smiled back. Instead, she pressed a hand on his hip and pressed gently, much like she had the day before. And, just like he had the day before, he winced.

She gave him a sweet smile. 'How's your hip feeling?'

'Oh, aren't you hilarious?'

'I'm not the one trying to be a comedian this morning.'

'I wouldn't have had to be anything besides asleep if you hadn't woken me up.' Now he ran a hand over the back of his neck, pushing his chest out ever so slightly. She swallowed. 'What time is it?'

'I... I don't know,' Jess replied as she realised she didn't. She winced. 'I'm sorry for waking you up. I just didn't know what to do...' She waited a beat. 'Thank you. For your help.'

He nodded. 'You have a burst pipe?'

'Your guess is as good as mine. All I know is that I woke up with water dripping onto my face.' She sighed. 'The house is a mess.'

It would be a logistical nightmare for her. Not because she would have to take care of getting it fixed, but because she wasn't only staying at Anja's house to house-sit. No, she had just bought her own place and was staying at Anja's until her new home could be made liveable. It was small, and the deposit had taken most of her savings, but it was her own. A fact that always, always brought her joy.

It reminded her that when she'd cut ties with her parents two years ago she had nothing except her university degree. It could have been enough, especially since her surname meant something in the finance industry she'd been trained for, but she hadn't wanted to rely on that. She wanted something of her *own*. Something that couldn't in any way be attributed to her rich, successful parents whose only concern had been their business.

Not the child they'd mistakenly conceived.

So she'd applied for a job she was wholly overqualified for, doing the day-to-day admin for a yoga studio. She updated and maintained Anja's website, managed bookings, dealt with queries, emails and, for the past year, helped Anja with the admin for opening her studio in Sydney. It had been a dream of Anja's as Chet was Australian and she'd wanted roots there just like Chet had in South Africa.

And the job had turned out to be a dream for Jess—the constant stream of things to do a welcome distraction from the past and the parents she'd walked away from.

For two years Jess hadn't spent any of the money she'd earned on anything besides the essentials. It meant that she was able to afford the small flat she'd bought, twenty minutes away from Chet and Anja's place. But that flat was a mess.

She couldn't begrudge it since its state was why she'd got it at such a good price, but it needed a lot of work before anyone could live there. Since Chet owned a construction company he'd offered to do the work for her, and had refused payment. And then Anja had found out Jess's lease was ending and her landlord was being difficult about letting her stay there on a month-to-month contract and had offered for Jess to stay at their place until her flat was habitable.

She knew they felt indebted to her. Especially since *she'd* refused to consider payment for carrying their child. But really, she saw them as family. As the only family she had. And family did things like that for one another. They cared, and helped, and sacrificed. Not because they wanted anything in return, but because they loved one another.

The concept was foreign to her parents, and that was part of the reason she hadn't spoken to them in two years. But it was okay. She'd found her place.

Except in the literal sense, since her place was currently flooded.

She sighed again. 'I should probably call Anja. Excuse me.'

'There's not much she can do from there.'

'Maybe not, but I still need to tell her before I start sorting it all out.'

'Sure,' he agreed. 'Or, if you give me a moment to put on a shirt, I can have a look and help you sort it out. So when you *do* call Anja you'll be calling her with answers, not just a problem.'

Relief swept through her first, and then came the niggling suspicion. Why was he offering to help her? What would he get from it?

'You're trying to get back on Anja's good side again, aren't you?'

'Isn't that why I do everything?' he replied dryly, making her wonder what he really meant. Dozens of options went through her head but, for the life of her, she couldn't focus on one of them. Realising it meant that she was tired, that she needed help, Jess nodded.

'I'd appreciate the help. Thanks.'

'I'll see you in a minute.'

She watched as he jogged back to his house, taking in the way his jeans rode low on his hips. It gave her the perfect view of a very fine butt, and a muscular back just asking her to run her hands over it.

Jess tried to ignore the way her body responded to the idea, but then she realised that Dylan wearing jeans to bed didn't make sense. If he didn't wear a shirt, he definitely wouldn't wear jeans. Which meant that he must have just thrown on the first thing that had been close by…and that he probably didn't wear any pants to bed either…

The image sent her thoughts down a dangerous road, and suddenly she couldn't stop imagining what Dylan would look like naked. Or what it would feel like to be in that bed with him, turning over during the night to run her hands over that delicious body of his. To snuggle closer and kiss him, to feel the way his body responded to hers. With him naked, there would be no barrier to what would happen next, and she'd be able to—

'Jess?' She jumped and felt her cheeks flush when she saw Dylan in front of her, completely clothed, with a puzzled look on his face. 'Are you okay?'

'Yeah, I'm fine. Ready to go inside?' She didn't wait for his answer and instead walked to the house.

Where had *that* come from? she thought. She wasn't the kind of girl who had fantasies about men she barely knew. Hell, she didn't have fantasies about men at all. She'd never been the type. She hadn't felt the need to date around and see where it would take her. She'd had two steady boyfriends in her life, and both relationships had only lasted about a year.

When her last relationship had ended, Jess had seen no point in trying again. Sure, it might have been because her life had completely changed shortly after the break-up. But she'd worked hard to rebuild it—by herself—for the last two years and she hadn't seen the point in having a man around while she did.

So perhaps the fantasy she'd just had about Dylan was the result of the nothingness she'd had in her life since she'd broken up with her last boyfriend. Or it could have been her over-excited pregnancy hormones. She would put it down to both, and refuse to acknowledge the third option.

That maybe she just *wanted* her best friend's brother.

She was almost relieved when she saw the puddles on the floor when she walked in. It gave her something else to think about. Something else to worry about.

'Wow,' he said from behind her.

'Yeah,' she replied, taking it all in. 'I'm not sure what happened.'

'It looks like it came from the second floor. I'll go take a look.'

While he was upstairs, Jess tried to do some damage control. She used towels to soak up the water on the floor, and wiped all the surfaces that had been affected. Fortunately, it seemed the water had only leaked in her bedroom, the kitchen and onto the passage that led to the front door, missing the carpeted lounge and its expensive furniture.

But she was still out of breath when Dylan returned.

'It looks like a geyser burst. A quick fix, though I'm not sure we can say the same for the ceiling. There's some water damage—' He broke off and frowned at her. 'Are you okay?'

'Yeah, fine.' She waved a hand. 'I'm just not used to not being able to do normal things like dry the floor.'

'Why don't you rest for a bit? I'll finish up here and make the necessary calls.'

'No, you don't have to.'

She stepped onto the towel in front of her to pick up the one just beyond it, but it slipped under her feet and she felt herself falling before she fully realised what was happening. A strong arm went around her waist and drew her up, and then Jess found herself staring into Dylan's eyes.

There was concern there, but she could also see the faint light of anger at her refusal. But seconds passed and neither of them looked away, and soon his eyes changed. The concern, the anger, faded and was slowly replaced by interest.

By attraction.

That was the word for it, she thought. And it

was a dangerous thought since something instantly sprang inside her chest at the prospect, at the recognition of what had caused her fantasy about Dylan earlier. She swallowed as the attraction changed to desire, and more seconds passed as she realised that that change was because of whatever he saw in *her* eyes.

Because being reminded about the fantasy she'd had about him earlier had made her body go hot. Had made her tingle, ache. Now she was pressed against the chest she'd spent days admiring, her hands braced against it, and she could feel his heart thudding against her hand. She should move, she told herself.

But she couldn't bring herself to put distance between them. The only movement she wanted to act on was to press herself even closer against him. To feel his muscular body tight against her, and have him feel the softness of her body. Her belly would get in the way, but she could—

The thought stopped her imagination abruptly, and shame took the place of desire. How *could* she be thinking these things when she was *pregnant*? When she was carrying a member of Dylan's family?

There was no way she could entertain these fantasies. She couldn't think about Dylan in any way other than as Anja's brother, the uncle to the child she carried. Getting involved with him had no benefits. It would probably hurt her best friend. It might even hurt the baby.

And though she wasn't the biological mother, while she carried him or her, *she* was responsible for the baby. *The baby* was her most important priority, and she couldn't ignore that just because Dylan made her feel things she'd forgotten she could feel.

Her relationship with Anja was important to her. More important than anything else. She would *not* screw it up. 'Thanks,' she murmured, thoroughly doused of the heat of attraction. 'Why don't you get this cleared up and I'll make the calls? I have the information on my laptop.'

'It's not damaged?' he asked her quietly, taking a step away from her.

'It's in the lounge. The water didn't get there.'

'Okay then.'

With careful steps, Jess made her way to the lounge. There would be no repeat performance of the last ten minutes.

Not now, not ever.

CHAPTER FOUR

BY THE TIME Dylan was done clearing up, the plumber had arrived and confirmed his suspicions: the geyser *had* burst. While they liaised with the insurance company and arranged for it to be replaced and informed them of the other damage, Dylan watched Jess. She'd been acting strangely from the moment he'd answered the door that morning, and he couldn't quite figure out why.

Was it because of the way things had ended between them the day before? Maybe, he thought. But then he remembered the way things had crackled between them when he'd saved her from falling. The way his body had reacted to her body's proximity, and the shame he'd felt when she'd pulled away.

She was pregnant, for crying out loud. There was no circumstance in which that didn't make her off-limits. He needed to remember that, he thought, when his heart stuttered as his eyes rested on her.

But, damn it, there was just *something* about her that pulled him in. That made rational thought not matter, and made hope flair when it shouldn't. And it had nothing to do with her relationship with his sister.

He told himself to pull back, to control himself, and went over to talk with her.

'The insurance is sending out their own evaluators this afternoon,' she said, and he saw the fatigue in her eyes.

'Figured as much when we realised the plumber we called wasn't on their list of approved service providers.'

'I've told them what the plumber identified the problem as, and gave them the details of the geyser. I doubt they'll arrive with it—wouldn't want to waste their money in case it wasn't what we said—but it should be replaced by the end of the day.'

'And the ceiling?'

'They're sending someone out for that and the rest of the damage today, too.'

He nodded. 'I don't think the ceiling will be too much of an effort. Might just be a paint job. The rest will have to dry.'

'It'll probably take a good solid two days,' she replied. 'And the water will probably be off for today. The painting should be done tomorrow, but the fumes might keep me out for at least another day.' She bit her lip. 'It might end up being more than two days.' She rested a hand on her stomach, and the action did something strange to his insides.

'Do you have somewhere to go?' he asked, his thoughts making his words gruff.

'No,' she said softly.

'Where do you live when you're not living here?'

'I just bought a place that isn't ready for me to move in yet. And the lease of the one I rented before is up.' She sighed. 'Anja and Chet are letting me stay here until my flat's ready.'

He processed the information. 'What about the father of the baby?'

She hesitated. 'He isn't an option right now.'

'So he doesn't care where the mother of his child is?'

'That's not—' She broke off. 'He isn't an option. But this isn't your problem, so don't worry. I'll figure something out.'

'I *will* worry. You have nowhere to go.'

'I'll be fine.'

'Jess—'

'Why are you pushing me?'

'Why won't you accept my help?'

'I *have* accepted your help. With all of this.' She waved her hand around them at the house. 'You've done enough.'

'Not if I leave you to figure things out by yourself,' he argued. 'Letting someone help you isn't going to rob you of anything, you know.'

'Not in my experience.'

He paused. 'What do you mean?'

'Nothing,' she said immediately, shaking her head. 'It doesn't mean anything.'

He studied her. Couldn't bring himself to look away from her. Not when her expression was so captivating. She'd been hurt before, he saw. And realised that hurt had made her lose something of herself.

Though he barely knew her, Dylan found his fists curling and his mind fantasising about being alone with whoever had hurt her. And since she was pregnant and didn't want to turn to the father of her child for help, Dylan was willing to bet he knew who he'd like to hurt.

He forced himself to relax. 'Okay, how about you get some of your clothes and come over to my place for breakfast? You can figure it out there,' he added over the protest he could sense would come from her.

But, instead of protesting, she said, 'That would be great, thanks,' surprising him. He watched as she got up—resisting the urge to help her when her movements looked the slightest bit sluggish—and waited in the passage leading to the front door while she packed.

He used the time to look at his sister's house. Just as he'd told Jess the day before, he preferred the décor here to that of his own house. Though the architecture was much the same, the bright colours made Anja's house look more homely than his own. When he'd told Anja as much, she'd told him that if he'd been there, maybe he could have made sure his was homely, too.

It had been the first sign of the crack in their relationship, but of course, he'd ignored it. It had been easier to do than facing the fact that he should have been home…

Jess came out then, just in time to stop those thoughts from spiralling. He wordlessly took the small suitcase she had, and turned towards his place. He was almost surprised to see how sullen the sky had become, though he shouldn't have been. It was autumn, and the warmth of the past few days had been more of a fluke than the grey sky.

He opened the door of his house to an excited dog, who became even more excited when she saw Jess behind him. Though he could still see the fatigue in Jess's eyes, she dutifully gave Daisy the attention the dog wanted and then followed him into the kitchen.

It was strange having her in his house again. Which itself was strange, considering that he'd only been living in that house for eight days him-

self after being away from it for two years. And
since the décor had changed while he'd been
away, it was almost like living in a new place.

'You can have the guest room,' he told her,
leading the way. 'My housekeeper comes in
every second day, so the room should be okay
to stay in. There's an en suite bathroom, too, so
it has everything you need.'

'Thanks. I think I'll take a shower and change.'

'And I'll get breakfast ready.'

'Oh, you really don't have to—'

'I know,' he interrupted her. 'But I'm hungry,
too, so it won't be that much of an effort.'

He left before she could argue with him, and
started making their breakfast. Cooking was
one of the habits he'd picked up growing up that
didn't annoy him. At first it had been for sur-
vival. After it had become clear his father wasn't
going to come home, his mother had given up
on most tasks, including feeding them.

So Dylan had used the money he'd found in
his father's safe to buy food, but he'd quickly
realised that the money wouldn't last if he didn't
learn how to buy sustainable items. And that
the items that *had* been sustainable required
effort on his behalf. So he'd spent a lot of time
watching cooking shows, had flipped through
the faded cookbooks in his mother's bookshelf
and had taught himself to cook. He'd soon re-

alised that it calmed him, and had roped Anja in, hoping she'd feel the same way.

'You look better,' he said when he saw Jess walk into the kitchen. He plated the muffins his housekeeper had made.

'You mean better than the horror show I was this morning?'

'Not at all. I just meant—' He broke off when he saw her smile, and felt his stomach flip. He ignored it.

'Do you want something to drink?'

'Tea, please.' She settled onto the bar stool at the counter.

'I have more comfortable chairs in the living room.'

'I know. But I won't let this baby rob me of the opportunity to eat while I watch you cook.'

She gave him a cheeky grin, and he laughed. She *did* look better than before. Not only because now she wore a long-sleeved black dress that stretched down to her feet with a belt tied under her breasts accentuating her bump, but because she didn't look quite as tired, as restless, as she had when she'd first got there.

He wondered if that meant he could convince her to stay with him while the work on Anja's house was being done. The thought was as surprising as it was sudden, but when he thought about it he realised it wouldn't be such a bad idea.

Unless he thought about how things sparked between them. And how badly he wanted to kiss her lips, to taste her mouth and feel the fullness of her body against his again...

Which, of course, he wouldn't think about.

He told himself to wait until breakfast was over before he mentioned it, and slid the tea and muffins in front of her. 'Your wish is my command.'

'You're such a good man,' she breathed as she picked up a chocolate muffin.

He bit back a grin. 'Those are the first ones I go for, too.'

'They're delicious. Where did you get them?'

'My housekeeper made them for me.'

'They're *homemade*? You need to ask her for the recipe.'

'You cook?' he asked, and started cutting fruit. He didn't know what was in a pregnant woman's diet, but he figured he'd cover all his bases.

'That's *baking*, Dylan.'

'You bake?'

'No.'

His lips curved. 'So you cook, then?'

'Nope.'

'Then why did you correct me?'

'It seemed like a fun thing to do,' she said with a smile, and then sobered. 'I've been learning how to do both over the last few years. I'm not quite at the level of being able to say that I can cook or bake *well*, but I can feed myself. And these—' she lifted the muffin '—are definitely the kind of food I'd like to learn how to make.'

'What happened a few years ago? That made you want to learn how to cook and bake, I mean.' He set the fruit he'd been cutting up to the side, and began preparing the bacon and eggs.

'I... I moved out of my parents' house.'

He frowned. 'How old are you?'

'Old enough to have been out of my parents' house by then,' she said with a laugh, but it sounded forced. 'We used to have a cook, so there was never really a need for me to learn how to feed myself.'

'You had a cook?'

'Yes.' He glanced over to see the hesitation in her eyes. 'Extravagant, isn't it?'

'I wasn't thinking that.'

'I wouldn't blame you if you did.'

He turned to her and watched as she avoided his eyes. And suddenly he thought that perhaps he'd attributed the hurt he saw in her to someone who hadn't deserved it.

'So you had an...extravagant childhood?'

'I guess you could say that.'

'What would you say?'

'I...was always well provided for.' He could hear the care she'd taken with those words.

'Your parents are wealthy?'

'Yes.'

'So why—' He broke off, knowing that his question would veer into territory she might not be comfortable with. But she finished his sentence for him.

'Why am I working as a PA?' He nodded. 'Well, I wasn't...well cared for. Or cared for at all,' she added softly, and Dylan felt his heart throb. 'So, when I moved out, I stopped talking to them. Which meant I had to take care of myself, hence this job.'

Seconds passed as he digested this new information. 'When you didn't want my help this morning, were you...thinking about them?'

'Only about how they used to throw it in my face whenever I asked them for help.' She paused. 'I remember when I was younger, I started saving for a new laptop. I didn't want to use my dad's old one any more, so I got a job and put away every cent of it so I could buy myself a new one. But my dad's laptop broke before I had enough money to replace it, so I asked them to help me buy a new one.' She lifted a hand, brushed at something on her cheek that he couldn't see. 'I thought that having half of the money for it—that working for it—would make them proud, but—' she cleared her throat '—but it didn't. They helped me buy the laptop, and reminded me of it whenever I acted in a way they didn't approve of.'

He blew out a breath, his heart aching when he saw the fear on Jess's face. Fear he realised came from telling him something so intimate. 'I'm sorry, Jess.'

'Don't be,' she said, avoiding his eyes. 'It's not your fault.'

But still, silence stretched long and awkwardly between them.

Dylan wished he could find something to say to make her feel better. Clearly, she'd had a tough time growing up just like he'd had. So, in fact, he should have known *exactly* what to say to her.

But, instead of helping him to find words of comfort, that fact kept him silent. Because he *did* know how awful it was, and that meant that nothing he could say would make her feel any better. And though he'd only met Jess the day before, something told him she wasn't the kind of person who wanted fake consolation.

He appreciated that. Respected it.

And yet, when he looked at her again, he heard himself saying, 'I guess you and I have more in common than I thought.'

CHAPTER FIVE

'SEEMS LIKE IT,' Jess replied, and wondered why that suddenly mattered. Wondered why she wasn't alarmed by the fact that it did.

Perhaps it was because she couldn't deny how much…better she felt immediately after he said it. It made her feel like less of a fool for bringing up the subject of her parents when she knew she shouldn't have. When she knew that doing so would bring out that side of her that was bitter and resentful.

That *hurt*.

It left a terrible taste in her throat, and Jess drank desperately from her tea to try to take it away. Even though her mind told her the response was irrational. Even though she knew that that taste was imaginary.

Damn her parents for doing this to her, she thought. She squeezed her eyes shut, and then forced herself to open them again. When she did, she saw that Dylan was watching her. Heat rushed to her cheeks, and the air in her lungs grew terribly heavy.

'I'm sorry that they hurt you,' he said.

'It doesn't matter.'

'But they did.'

'And yours hurt you,' she replied primly. 'We survive.'

'Do we?' he asked with a half-smile. 'Do you think we're surviving?'

'You don't?'

'I…don't just want to survive if this is surviving,' he admitted quietly. 'If constantly worrying that I'm repeating the mistakes of my parents—that I'm disappointing the people I love—is surviving.'

'I…feel the same,' she said in surprise. 'About surviving.'

He didn't reply for a moment. 'When I was on the second floor of Anja's house earlier I noticed something strange.' He turned back to the stove and flipped an egg.

Confusion spread through her, but the change in topic and the fact that he wasn't looking at her any more had the breath in her lungs moving easily again. 'Yeah?' she replied, grateful that her voice wasn't nearly as shaky as she'd thought it would be.

She took a deep breath, and then busied herself with adding fruit and yoghurt to a bowl.

'Yeah. A chair,' he said, deadpan, and her hand froze. 'In front of a window.'

She forced herself to move. 'That *is* strange.'

'Overlooking my property.'

'Even stranger.' She set the bowl down in front of her and dug in.

She couldn't admit her guilt if she couldn't speak.

'I thought so,' he continued conversationally. 'Until I realised that that was the window you pointed out to me yesterday. Where you said you saw me fall from.'

'Was it?'

'*And* then I remembered you'd known I'd been here for a week.'

She pretended to think about it. 'I don't remember. Sorry, pregnancy brain.'

'Pity.'

Dylan set two plates—one with bacon, one with the eggs—on the counter with the rest of the food, and then took a third and began dishing for himself. As he settled on the stool next to her, Jess tried to think of something to say to change the topic of conversation.

Except she couldn't think of anything. All she *could* think about was the fact that he knew. He *knew* she'd been watching him.

She rolled her eyes. Sighed. 'Okay, yes, fine. That's where I was watching you from.'

He lifted his eyebrows and didn't say anything.

Damn it! Why was that so *sexy*?

'I mean, I didn't know it was you. Doesn't that count for something?'

He cocked his head. 'You mean towards the imaginary scoreboard that gives you points for being a pervert?'

'I am *not*—' She cut off her own protest when she saw the amusement in his eyes. 'What would you have done if I was working outside in my bikini?'

'Would it make you feel better if I said I'd watch?'

'Yes.' She sniffed. 'Yes, it would.'

'Then I'd have watched.'

She couldn't resist her own amusement at the expression on his face now. 'With chips?'

'You watched me…with chips?'

'Yesterday it was chips.' She considered her next words. *What the hell?* 'The day before it was popcorn. And the day before that, chocolate.'

'Choc…' he said before realisation dawned. 'How many days have you been watching me?'

'Don't act coy now,' she replied. 'I told you you'd been home for at least a week, so that's how many days I've been watching you.'

There was a beat of silence before his face split

into a smile and laughter spilled from his lips. It made him look younger, more carefree, and Jess realised how little of either of those his expression normally held. She thought about his earlier words—about what he'd said about surviving—and for the first time Jess felt sorry for her best friend's brother.

It had been easy to see Dylan as the unfeeling older brother who'd left his grieving mother and sister weeks after they'd buried their father. Easy because she'd only heard Anja's side of things. Because she'd only seen the aftermath of Dylan's departure.

But now, after the time—however short—she'd spent with Dylan, Jess finally considered the other side of the story. That clearly told her that her rash judgement was undeserved. She only had to look at Dylan's face when he wasn't laughing to realise it.

'I'm glad you find it so funny,' she managed, though her thoughts made it sound more serious than she'd intended.

'You don't?' he asked, immediately sobering.

'No, no, I do.' She forced a smile, but could tell he wasn't buying it. 'I'm sorry, I just… I just remembered I spoke with Anja this morning.'

It was the first thing she could think of to say. And when the words changed the air between

ranging where I'll stay while the whole thing next door is going on.'

'Of course you can.'

He stood with her—awkwardly, she thought, even though that word didn't really fit with a man who looked like Dylan.

'I'll see you in a bit,' she said, and then walked back to the room and felt her body sag with relief when she lay on the bed. It had been a tiring morning. Being pregnant had made it worse, but she suspected she would have felt that way even if she hadn't been pregnant.

But the fact that her thoughts and emotions were all over the place she *would* blame on her pregnancy. It was the only logical explanation for the disappointment that still lingered. It was the only way she could explain why Dylan made her feel the way he did. And why meeting him had made her think so much of her own family.

She hadn't been lying when she'd told him she respected that he wanted a relationship with Anja again. But she couldn't quite understand it. Not when she didn't have anything to compare it to. She felt absolutely no desire to repair her relationship with her parents. She didn't think they deserved her in their lives, and she sure as hell didn't think she deserved *them*. And if their actions—or lack thereof—since she'd moved out told her anything, it was that they didn't want to repair their relationship with her either.

Maybe that was why she'd felt so disappointed by what Dylan had told her. Because it had been a reminder of what Jess *didn't* have—a family who would fight for her.

She suddenly hoped Anja would give Dylan a chance. Her friend had gone deathly silent the day before when Jess had first called to tell her about Dylan's arrival. And then she'd politely thanked Jess and put down the phone.

When Jess had called that morning, her reaction had been similar, though this time Anja had told her she would try to come home sooner and had asked Jess not to tell Dylan anything about the baby.

It was a fair request. In fact, Jess had fully intended not to say anything to Dylan about the baby. She would let Anja deal with that. After all, it was none of Jess's business.

Except that Jess *wanted* to tell Dylan. It felt wrong not to. Or, more accurately, Jess told herself quickly, she wanted *Anja* to tell Dylan. Sooner, rather than later. Because not all families wanted to fight to stay a family. That was special. But some things—some decisions—could break a family so completely that it couldn't be fixed, even if someone wanted to fight for it.

She didn't think Dylan leaving was that thing, that decision. Especially since she suspected that he'd left for reasons neither she nor Anja knew. Good reasons. But keeping this child a secret from him—keeping the circumstances around the child's conception a secret—might just be...

It exhausted her to think about it and she closed her eyes, pushing the thoughts and emotions away. She wouldn't let Dylan's demons keep her from sleeping.

She certainly wouldn't let her own demons do that either.

CHAPTER SIX

D<small>YLAN LOOKED UP</small> from the book that he was reading when Daisy lifted her head from where it rested on his leg and lumbered off the couch. His heart did something strange in his chest when he saw it was because Jess had walked into his living room, looking just as sleepy and mussed and sexy as she had when he'd opened his door to her that morning.

It didn't seem fair that she could do something strange to his heart when the way she looked was entirely by accident. When the waves of her hair just always seemed to be mussed, when the sleepiness was an unavoidable consequence of waking up.

As for the sexiness… Well, he didn't think she intended to make him think of her that way. Nor did he think she intended to make him picture how she'd look waking up in his bed. How imagining it made his body tighten with a need he didn't understand. With a need he *didn't want*.

'Sleep well?' he asked gruffly.

'Yeah, thanks. Sorry that it was so long.'

'It wasn't.'

'The insurance?'

'The plumbers have come and gone. The ceiling people called to say they'd only be able to make it out tomorrow. You left your phone on the kitchen counter,' he said at her confused look.

She nodded but didn't reply, and the only sound between them was Daisy's attempts to get Jess to rub her belly. He watched as Jess lowered to her haunches and then slowly sat down on the carpet over the wooden floor. With one hand on her own stomach, she gave Daisy what she wanted and the simple image again did strange things to Dylan's heart.

It made absolutely no sense.

How did a woman he barely knew have such a powerful effect on him? A woman who was clearly off-limits? Who was pregnant? Who was his sister's friend?

And yet Jess affected him. She *tempted* him. More than just physically, too. The picture in front of him made him *want*. And what it made him want was even more baffling because he'd never, ever thought about it before.

Family.

Seeing Jess pregnant made him think about having a family. About having his own wife, his own child on the way. It wasn't something he'd ever wanted. His family situation had taught him that some people weren't meant to have children. They weren't meant to be parents.

He wasn't his mother. He wouldn't knowingly bring a child into the world knowing the brokenness of the situation they'd be born into. And he *was* broken. Not as much as his father—his mother, maybe—but he certainly wasn't whole enough to become a father himself.

Which was why considering it made absolutely no sense.

He set his book aside, told himself it was being in the house, being with Jess that was driving him to insanity. 'I'm going for a walk,' he told her, and moved towards the front door.

'Can I come with you?' she asked from behind him and he turned, frowning.

'Why?'

'It's going to rain soon.' She pointedly looked out of the glass doors where the sky was dark, warning of what was about to come. 'I won't have a chance to do it in a while and I feel—' Her eyes went soft, almost apologetic.

'You feel what?'

'Suffocated.'

He lifted his brows. 'By me? Because then you probably shouldn't take a walk with me.'

'It's not you.'

It was the only answer she offered and he sighed. Nodded. She lifted her arms in response and, after a brief moment of hesitation, he strode forward and helped her up. He resented the heat that went through his body at her proximity and stepped away from her as soon as he knew she was steady.

And then he whistled to Daisy and the three of them made their way to one of the most important places of his childhood.

Once, there had been one large house on the property where he and Anja lived. They'd grown up there, and when they'd got older and their mother had moved to be closer to her family, Anja and Dylan had stayed.

'You're lucky,' Jess said from beside him as they walked the pathway to the large forest that stood just behind his property. 'I would have killed to have this in my backyard.'

'I *am* lucky,' he agreed. 'It's because of Anja.'

'What do you mean?'

'We lived here as kids, and she—'

'Wait, what?' He looked over to see confusion on her face. 'You lived here as kids? In… your house?'

'Our houses weren't always on adjacent properties. There used to be one large property, with one large house on it, where we grew up. But we tore the house down when my mother moved to Langebaan and built two separate houses instead.'

She nodded, but didn't respond as they made their way through the forest path he'd taken so many times as a child. The trees were tall and full, the kind that had always made him feel as if he was in a movie of some sort. Daisy immediately sprinted out of sight—as she always did—and she'd find him again as soon as he'd call to her on their way back.

'Why did you say you had this because of Anja?'

'Because she…she wanted me to have it.' His heart ached at the reminder of how generous she'd been. 'When we split the property, she was adamant that I have the pathway. That I have easy access to this place.' His feet faltered just as he passed the tree where his sister had once carved her initials. It was almost as if his feet knew he was talking about her. He forced them forward.

'It was special to you,' Jess said in that understanding way she had. 'To both of you.'

He cleared his throat. 'Yeah. We came here a lot as children. Well, until Anja stopped coming with me because I used to scare her so often.' His lips curled at the memory. 'She told me the place reminded her of a horror movie she'd watched, so how could I resist?'

Jess smiled. 'Naturally.'

'Anyway, after she stopped coming… I used to use this place to think. To…escape.'

'Escape?'

'From the responsibility of looking after my family.' His throat burned with emotion. 'Sounds terrible, doesn't it?'

'How old were you?'

'Fourteen.'

'Then no,' she said. 'It doesn't sound terrible for a fourteen-year-old not to want the responsibility of a family.' She paused. 'Your father left when you were fourteen?'

Of course she knew they'd been abandoned, he thought. She was his sister's best friend. A fact he conveniently seemed to forget.

'Yes.' He paused. 'What did she tell you about it?'

'Not much.' They stopped exactly where he'd stopped all those years ago—at the hilltop overlooking the busy hub of central Cape Town. Where he would dream about a life where his parents weren't such complete disasters. And he hadn't even known then what he knew now about his mother. 'Just that he had an…addiction and he left because of it.'

He nodded and let her words sit between them while he thought about what to say.

'It's beautiful,' Jess breathed after a moment,

and he felt her pleasure soothe some of the hurt that always accompanied thoughts of his past. He could almost forget then that she'd been a part of the reason he'd wanted to come to this place initially. To get away from...*her* and everything she made him feel. But now he thought it was...nice that she was there with him.

What was *happening* to him?

'It is, isn't it?' he said instead of pondering the disturbing thoughts that had popped into his head. But they were only replaced by more disturbing thoughts—by what they'd been talking about earlier—and he heard himself speak before his mind had fully caught up with the words he was saying.

'I always thought it was strange that Anja wanted to live here.'

'You didn't?'

'No. The house...didn't exactly have the best memories for us. But the place did. *This* place did,' he added, gesturing around them. 'So we told ourselves that we'd save that and tear down the rest. Build something new.' He ran a hand through his hair. 'It was round about the same time Anja met Chet, and she was convinced pretty early on that they were going to be married. So, instead of building another big house, we settled for two.' He paused. 'Didn't you ever wonder why they look so similar? We had the same architect.'

'Actually, I hadn't noticed.'

He noted the tone of her voice. 'Anja didn't tell you about any of this?'

She shook her head, the expression on her face reflecting the tone. 'She's pretty tight-lipped about some things.'

'Me, you mean,' he offered when it was clear she wouldn't say it.

'No. Well, not only you,' she said when he gave her a doubtful look. 'She's told me the major things. But the details…she didn't really offer them, and I never wanted to ask.'

'Why not?'

'I…' She faltered. Frowned. 'I guess I didn't want to push her to talk about something she didn't want to talk about.'

'Sometimes we need to be pushed to talk about the things we don't want to talk about.'

'So I should force you to talk about why you left?' she shot back, eyes troubled, and then she immediately shook her head. 'No, I'm sorry. I shouldn't have said that.'

'No, you shouldn't have,' he replied. 'Not because you're wrong—you're not—but you sounded…defensive.'

'No.'

'No?' he repeated. 'No, you didn't sound defensive? Or no, you're not allowing me to call you out on sounding defensive?' She didn't answer him and he sighed. 'Jess—'

'You're right,' she said with a slight laugh. 'I'm being defensive because I'm defending my decision not to push my friend to tell me something just in case it ends up pushing her away. From me.'

Realising the enormity of what she'd just admitted—to him, to herself—Dylan said, 'She probably didn't tell you about the house because you didn't push. Because you knew not to push.'

'I...don't understand.'

'But you do. The fact that you don't ask her about it means you understand,' he told her. 'Anja wanted a clean start. We both did. So, new houses and no talk of the past.' He gestured for Jess to sit down and, after he'd helped her, he settled down himself, their legs dangling over the hill.

'It's easier that way,' she said. 'Except, for some reason, we keep talking about our pasts with one another.'

He didn't reply. Chose not to since all he wanted to say was that it made no sense. Nothing about what was happening between them made sense. All Dylan knew was that he felt as if he'd been caught in an alternate reality where it didn't *have* to make sense. Where all the reasons why sharing with Jess—why getting to know her—was a bad idea ceased to exist.

A voice inside his head screamed that he didn't want this. And yet he found it *easy* to ignore it.

And felt himself sink deeper.

'You told Anja about your parents, didn't you?'

'Yeah, she knows.'

'Good.'

'Good?' she repeated. 'Why's that good?'

'You shouldn't keep it to yourself.'

'I haven't been,' she said wryly. 'I've shared more with you than I ever have with Anja.'

'You…have?'

She gave a soft laugh that went right through him. 'She doesn't know about the laptop thing. Or that they used to hold things like that against me. She only knows that they were…bad parents. That the money made them worse.' She paused. 'Or maybe it's just easier for me to blame the money instead of who they are.'

'There's more.'

'Isn't there always?' she asked with a small smile. 'But you get the picture.' She lifted a shoulder.

He reached out and took her hand, and only really realised he had when she flipped hers over and threaded her fingers through his. He didn't know how long they sat like that, but he *did* know that it felt *good*. That for the first time in a long time he didn't feel alone.

It had warmth spreading through his chest, even though he could acknowledge that it shouldn't have. Even though he could acknowledge that he should pull back, pull his hand from hers, before things could become more complicated. Before the alternate reality became his real one.

Instead, he said, 'I'm surprised you're being so nice to me, knowing what I've done.'

'And what's that?'

'Leaving.' He couldn't bring himself to look at her. 'Hurting Anja.'

'I'll admit, I didn't *want* to be nice to you.' Now he did look at her, and she gave him a small smile. 'I started working for Anja a couple of months after your father died. More than a month after you left.' Jess's free hand lifted, and she began to trace circles on her stomach. 'Of course, I didn't know that then. Anja was always professional with me, though I could sense that something was…off.' The circles grew larger. 'Then one day I found Anja crying and she told me about your father's death, and…how much she missed you.' Her hand stilled. Fell to her lap. 'I think that was the day our professional relationship changed into friendship. And I immediately took Anja's side in it all.'

'You should have. I've been a terrible brother.' Shame, guilt, anger washed through him. 'You *should* treat me like I'm a bad person.'

'But you're not.'

'I am to Anja.'

'No, Dylan. You just…hurt her. But you're a decent man, just like I told you this morning.' She squeezed his hand and then gently pulled hers out of his. He instantly felt a little emptier. 'And if I base my opinion of you on how you've treated me since we've met instead of what I thought I knew about you *before* we met, it's easy to be nice to you.'

'Even though I told you the way I've treated you might be because I want to get on Anja's good side?'

She laughed. 'Trust me, if you wanted to get on Anja's good side, being nice—or whatever it is you're being to me—would *not* be the way to go.'

'Why not?' Her expression changed, closed. 'Jess—'

'Do you plan on telling Anja why you left?' she said instead of answering his question. She didn't want to talk about it, he thought. Which he should respect. Even if it *was* strange that she'd drawn the line with that.

'Of course,' he replied, though he could hear the hesitation in his own tone. She nodded but didn't respond, and he watched as her hand went to her stomach again.

He frowned and, for the first time in a while, thought about her pregnancy. About the implications of her pregnancy. About how those implications meant he shouldn't have brought her to this place—to *his* place—which would, no doubt, always remind him of her whenever he came now. About how it meant that he shouldn't be talking to her like he hadn't to anyone else before, how he shouldn't allow himself to be comforted by her—to comfort *her*—when there was another man in her life.

Even if that man did appear to be absent for the moment.

'How has it been going?' he asked to keep himself from getting lost in the hope that thought brought. It was more urgent now, more pressing, and his mind had cleared enough for him to know he couldn't allow it to be.

'How has what been going?'

'Your pregnancy?'

'Oh, fine.' She waved a hand. 'I can't complain.'

'Can't? Or won't?'

She laughed softly. 'How is it that you can see through me so easily, Dylan?' The words felt like a punch in the stomach, but she didn't give him a chance to double over. 'I can't *and* won't complain. There are so many women out there who would love to be in my position.'

'Not entirely,' he murmured, and she gave him a confused look. 'I'm sorry, you probably don't want to be reminded of it.'

'I have no idea what you're talking about.'

She was going to make him say it, he thought, and sighed. 'You're pregnant and alone, Jess. You didn't even want to call to ask the father of your child for help this morning. I don't think that's a position many women want to be in.' He waited and then added, 'You don't have to pretend like it doesn't bother you.'

She blinked. And then she threw her head back and laughed. It sounded just as much in place in the forest as the birds he usually heard chirping in the trees. He wasn't sure what confused him more: that he'd thought that, or that she was laughing at her predicament.

'I didn't realise I'd made a joke,' he said stiffly.

'Oh, no, I'm sorry. I didn't mean to—' She broke off, bit her lip. And then she sighed, and the expression on her face changed to what he thought was resignation. 'I'm not pregnant and alone, Dylan. No man has abandoned me.'

'But—'

'I made you think that?' He nodded. 'Sorry. It's only because…it's complicated,' she said slowly. Seconds ticked by, turned into minutes, but neither of them spoke. Eventually Jess looked at him and something inside him flipped at the emotion in her eyes.

'Dylan…this baby…it isn't mine. I'm just… the surrogate.'

CHAPTER SEVEN

JESS HELD HER BREATH, hoping that she hadn't made a mistake. She knew she probably shouldn't have said anything to Dylan. But whatever it was that had her opening up to him—that had her telling him about her parents, that listened to his concerns about his past—had demanded that she tell him the truth. So had the part of her that had softened at his concern that she was going through her pregnancy alone.

It would be fine, she thought now, releasing her breath as she watched him. She wasn't betraying Anja by telling Dylan that she was a surrogate. As long as he didn't know that she was *Anja's* surrogate, it would be fine.

She hoped.

'You're...a surrogate?'

'That's what I said,' she replied lightly, hoping that it would defuse some of the tension between them.

'But...how? I mean, why?' Dylan shook his head and angled his body towards her.

'Well, I have a…friend who struggled to fall pregnant.' It was the best explanation she could offer.

'So you…offered to carry her child for her?'

She tilted her head, felt her heart sink. 'I did. Is that a problem?'

'No…no, it's not.' He lifted his eyes to hers. 'I'm not judging you, Jess.'

'Really? Because it really feels like you are.' And it was such a surprise that her throat felt clogged.

'It's just…a lot to take in.' Emotion crossed his face. 'I've never met…someone like you,' he said, looking away. 'I guess I'm struggling to understand why you'd do this to yourself.'

'Do what to myself?' Jess asked, cautioning herself to pull back when she wanted to snap the words at him. 'I get that you're trying to process this information, which is fine, I suppose, but you don't *have* to understand my choices.' She wanted to get up, storm off, but she knew she wouldn't be able to with her stomach in the way. She glanced down at the distance to the ground from where she was, and clenched her jaw. She couldn't risk it. 'Would you help me up? It looks like it's about to start raining and we should probably get back.'

He nodded and helped her up without a word. She felt even more annoyed when her skin prickled at his touch. When her body became so much more aware at his proximity.

But it gave her steam to storm off, and she walked ahead of him through the trees, leaving the buildings of Cape Town behind them.

It really was a beautiful place, she thought. And now that she knew how personal it was to him, she wondered why he'd let her tag along. Why had he told her things even Anja hadn't told her?

Why had *she* shared things with him? About her parents? She'd told him more about them than she'd ever told Anja. And why did she feel so disappointed by his reaction to finding out the baby she carried wasn't hers?

All of it worried her. And, just like she'd first thought when she'd met Dylan, it convinced her that she couldn't become involved with him. Or come between him and Anja. Anja was as close to family as she had, and she couldn't do anything to damage that. And she should probably stay away from Dylan if she kept that goal in mind.

Besides, she didn't *want* to become involved with Dylan…did she?

Just as she thought it there was a sudden clap of thunder, followed by the sound of rain. Not the steady, calming rainfall that often started rainy days, but a hard, angry downpour that had them both coming to a stop.

'I'm sorry,' Dylan said after a few moments. 'We should have left earlier.'

'Don't apologise,' she breathed, eyes on the rain. They were under the shield of the trees, which seemed to have formed some kind of canopy protecting them from the majority of the water. From where they stood, they could see the rain pouring down in front of them. 'It's all a part of the view.'

'I didn't quite anticipate this one,' he said with a soft laugh. 'Though it *is* something.' Neither of them spoke as the drops around them grew heavier.

'There's a part of me that wants to stay here until the storm is over.'

'Because you don't want to get wet?' Dylan asked, turning towards her.

'Because it's so beautiful. Angry, but beautiful.'

'Yeah, I know that feeling.'

Her eyes met his and she felt a shift in the air between them.

'What makes you think I'm angry?'

'Because of the way I responded to your… news back there.' His face tightened, but he didn't look away.

'It doesn't matter.'

'I think it does.'

His words stirred something in her chest, and she shook her head. 'It shouldn't. Our lives, our decisions, don't affect one another.' Though those lives, those decisions *did* seem to be intersecting, she thought. 'The smartest thing we can do is to remember that.'

Silence followed her words, and she felt the change in him before she saw it on his face.

'Are you always…smart, Jess?' he asked slowly, taking a step forward. Breaching the gap between them.

In her mind she stepped back, maintaining the distance that would ensure she wouldn't do something that would prove the exact opposite of her words.

In reality, her feet stayed exactly where they were.

'I like to think so,' she replied, her voice husky.

She wondered why, and then got the answer when she suddenly found herself pressed against Dylan's body. She swallowed, and a voice in her head desperately warned her that she couldn't make this mistake.

It warned her to move, to run, and get a room in a hotel as far away as possible from the man who held her in place with only his eyes.

But then the voice was muted by another, louder one in her mind. One that shouted only one thing.

Stay.

'I don't think I'm being very smart now.'

'With me?' Dylan asked, his eyes heating, his arms going around her. 'Should I be offended?'

'Not unless you think I'm wrong?' When he didn't reply, she nodded. 'I didn't think so.'

She kept her eyes on his as she brought her mouth closer, closer still, until finally their lips touched.

Jess felt thunder boom inside her at the contact. Felt it break something, and then, like the rain, that something poured through her body into her blood, rushing through her as she sank into the pleasure of kissing Dylan.

Because the man could *kiss*. There was no hesitation in the way his lips moved, no uncertainty in the way his tongue stole her breath. Her body trembled as her blood carried a headiness through her that she'd never felt before. As if its purpose had become more than to simply carry oxygen through her body. No, now it felt as if it carried thrills, sensations, *awareness* through her veins, and her hands tightened at Dylan's waist in response, as if they wanted to grip the feeling.

As if they wanted to capture it and never let go.

Dylan groaned as his hands moved over her body. Over the curves of her hips, her rounded belly, her breasts. They ached from his touch when his hands lingered, and then heated when he kneaded, softly, gently, adding more pressure each time so that the ache turned into longing, into desire, into *fire*.

He pressed her back until her feet hit a tree, the force of it sending a puddle of water right on their heads. But neither of them stopped. No, the coolness helped keep the fire at bay. Helped them start the kindling all over again.

Jess ran her hands over his back, over the muscles she'd admired ever since she'd first seen them in his backyard. Over the ridges she'd fantasised about. His shirt was plastered against his body from the water, and she moaned softly at how it saved her the trouble of going under his shirt to feel what she wanted.

Her fingers swept across the hardened planes, her hands moving from his back to his biceps, and then between them to his pecs.

It was so defined, so damn sexy that suddenly it felt as if she'd lost her breath, and she had to pull away so that she could breathe. His chest heaved as much as hers did as he rested his forehead against hers, and when their eyes met his lips curved into a smile that was the perfect illustration of what they'd just done.

Reckless. Spontaneous. Dangerous.

'It's raining,' she said huskily.

'Yeah, I know,' he replied with a soft chuckle. 'We both knew that before...*this* happened.'

'No, Dylan, I mean it's raining here, on us.' Just as she said it, drops splattered hard on both their faces. 'I don't think we can stay here any more.'

'No, we probably shouldn't.'

He took her hand and then whistled for Daisy. Seconds later, the dog came sprinting through the trees, wet and blissfully unaware of what her owner had just got up to. Together they ran for his house—although Jess couldn't quite call what she was doing running. But Dylan didn't seem to mind, and soon they were in the house, completely drenched.

'We should probably get out of these clothes,' she said, and felt her face burn as soon as she said it. 'I don't mean—'

'I know,' he said with a slight smile. Silence beat between them, and then he shook his head. 'But you're right. Besides, I should sort this little bugger out.'

He looked down at Daisy affectionately, and Jess felt something tumble in her chest. Not surprising, she thought, considering that everything inside her felt as if it had come apart.

'Dylan—'

'No, Jess,' he interrupted. 'We don't have to… talk about it.'

'I'd love to *not* talk about it,' she said with a bark of laughter. 'But how can we not? This— what just happened? It's not a good idea.'

'You think I don't know that?' Dylan answered, his expression serious.

'No, I'm sure you do,' she replied quietly, and felt fatigue seep back into her bones. 'So maybe you're right, and it's better that we don't talk about it.' Why did that make her so sad? 'I'm going to have a shower and then I'll call a hotel or something for the next few nights.'

'You can stay here.'

'No, I don't—'

'It won't happen again, Jess,' Dylan promised. 'And you being here is better. You'll be near if they need you next door. And you'll be able to call Anja if she needs to approve anything.'

They were good points, she knew, but still, agreeing felt like it would be the wrong decision. She didn't know how much of that was because her insides were still a mess from their kiss.

So she said, 'I'll think about it,' and walked to the room he'd shown her to that morning. She stripped off the wet clothing and showered quickly, and then dried the water from her hair before plaiting it and pinning the plaits around her head in a crown.

She pulled on thick woollen tights that she'd had the foresight to pack, and an oversized jersey that was just as thick, just as woollen. It made her look like an unshapen mess, but somehow that made her feel better. There was no way she would be tempted into seducing Dylan wearing that. No way he'd be tempted into seducing her either.

And because trying to find other accommodation seemed to require more energy than she had—along with going back out into the rain, getting the keys to her car, driving in the horrendous weather—her choice seemed to be made. She would stay there that night.

She should go out and tell him, she thought, but instead she climbed under the bedcovers, telling herself she would only rest for a moment. That she only needed comfort for a moment.

She'd made a mistake. Kissing Dylan had been a mistake. Because now that she knew what it felt like, she wanted more of it. And that wasn't an option.

She couldn't risk her friendship with Anja for more. It didn't matter that Dylan had been kind to her. That he'd listened to her. That it felt as if he understood her.

The attraction between them couldn't matter, nor the emotional connection. More than just being for Anja's sake, it was for *hers*, too. She didn't think that when Dylan found out whose baby she was carrying he'd understand why she'd kept it from him. Jess already knew that he'd be hurt because Anja hadn't told him about it, and she suspected *she* would be the target of the anger that hurt would turn into since he seemed so desperate to keep things civil with Anja.

It was easier to put some distance between them now, Jess told herself. Prevention was better than cure, and she needed to prevent the inevitable hurt that would come from entertaining anything other than a cordial relationship with Dylan.

Decided, she pulled the blankets closer around her and closed her eyes.

He was restless. Primed for a fight. Had been from the moment Jess had reminded him that their kiss was a bad idea.

The fact that she was right didn't have anything to do with it. No, he was upset because somehow she'd kept her mind when their kiss had made him lose his. When the kiss that *she'd* initiated had crossed the clear—albeit unspoken—boundaries between them, but *she'd* been the one to remind them of those boundaries after it had happened.

And yes, fine, maybe he'd wanted it to happen. Maybe he'd closed the distance between them in the forest because he'd wanted one of them to initiate a kiss. But he was only human. How was he supposed to resist the beauty, the vulnerability of her, wrapped up in that little bubble of anger? When that bubble had screamed of the passion he'd got to experience only minutes after he'd thought about it?

It all made him feel so edgy that he knew nothing good would come from facing Jess in that state. So, after he took care of Daisy, he peeled off his wet clothes and replaced them with gym clothes, and made his way to his home gym to expel some of the energy.

If it hadn't been raining, he'd go back to his task of chopping wood. It was laborious work, something that kept his mind and body busy. Something that distracted him from the fact that he should have gone to speak with his sister.

Unfortunately, now he could only seem to keep his body busy. No matter how hard he pushed himself during his cardio, his strength training, his thoughts kept looping back over the last few hours. Over his words, hers. Over her reactions, his.

He finished his workout, showered and went back downstairs. All the while, he was trying to figure out what he should say to her. The only thing that he came up with was an apology, but what would he be apologising for? For kissing her back? For enjoying it? For facing the fact that they'd made their lives infinitely more complicated by acknowledging their attraction to one another?

None of it made sense, but he knew he couldn't avoid her for ever, so he told himself to man up and went to find her. He wandered around the house, but she wasn't in the living room or the kitchen, and for one sick moment he worried that she'd left without telling him that she was going. As a last resort, he checked the guestroom and relief flooded through him when he saw the shape of her under the covers.

His eyes swept over her. Her face was flushed from the heat of sleep, her hair in some kind of plait pinned at the top of her head. A woollen-covered arm rested on her belly on top of the covers, rounding off a picture Dylan knew he wouldn't be able to push out of his head with ease.

He shut the door just as quickly as he'd opened it, careful not to make a sound and wake her, and put as much distance between him and the room as he could. Daisy looked up at him from her station in the corner of the kitchen when he walked in and whined when he leaned over the counter, his heart beating so fast he couldn't catch his breath.

What *was* that? he asked himself eventually. What was that burst of emotion in his chest at seeing her? What was the fierce protectiveness that had surged inside him?

Whatever it was, it wasn't welcome. And yet it wasn't unfamiliar. It took him some minutes, but the image of Jess sleeping had him realising why he'd reacted so uncharacteristically to her surrogacy news.

He felt *protective* of her. And he was worried that this pregnancy would somehow hurt her. That he wouldn't be able to keep her from getting hurt.

In some part of his brain he knew that it wasn't his job to protect her. Knew that his need to do so could only mean trouble. But he couldn't figure out why he still wanted to, despite knowing better.

He sucked in a breath. It was going to be a long night.

CHAPTER EIGHT

JESS FOUND DYLAN in front of the fire in his living room.

Rain thrashed against the glass doors, lightning flashed every few moments. Daisy was curled up next to Dylan on the couch, whining ever so softly every time thunder sounded. Jess didn't blame her. It seemed that they were experiencing one of the famous Cape Town storms, and if Jess had been Daisy she'd be curled up next to Dylan, too.

Except she wasn't Daisy, and she'd given herself a stern warning against thoughts like that. Reinforcing her resolve, she walked towards them slowly. Daisy popped her head up when she saw Jess, but Dylan kept staring into the fire. As though there was something he could see there that no one else could. As though it held all the answers to life's mysteries.

'Hey,' she said softly after a few more seconds. Daisy immediately jumped off the couch and rubbed herself against Jess and, obliging the dog, Jess gave her the attention she wanted. But her eyes were still on Dylan. Stayed on him, too, when his gaze met hers and she saw the pain there.

There was a long, long pause before it cleared and then he said, 'Hey.'

'Are you okay?'

'Fine,' he replied. 'You fell asleep.'

'Yeah, I did. Sorry. It's been more of an exciting day than I'm used to. Knocked me out.'

'That's fine.' He paused. 'Did you figure out what you're going to do?'

'I was hoping that your offer was still on the table.'

'Of course,' he told her, though his tone made her uncertain.

'Thanks.' She waited for him to say something more and, when he didn't, she added, 'I can be out tomorrow.'

'Why?'

'You just don't seem like you want me here.'

'No, it's not that.' He leaned forward now and drained the glass she hadn't noticed on the table in front of him. 'It's just been…an exciting day,' he repeated her words.

'That's true.' She fell silent and, rather than contemplate his strange mood, decided to channel her energy into something useful. 'Would you like me to make us something to eat?'

His brows rose. 'I thought you said you couldn't cook?'

'I said I only started to learn a few years ago. That's a lot of meals, Dylan, so I think I can make us a…pot of curry,' she said, improvising.

'You're going to make us…curry?'

'Why not?' She'd made it a couple of times before. She was pretty sure she could do it again. 'It's the perfect meal for this kind of weather.'

'Oh, I'm not arguing about that. I'm just wondering whether— No, you know what? I would love some curry.' He patted Daisy, who'd curled up next to him again when it became clear she wasn't going to get any more attention from Jess, and stood. 'Come on, I'll show you where everything is.'

Jess would have found it hard to describe the next hour. But she *was* sure that no one would mistake it for any kind of cooking show. *Especially* not with Dylan watching her every move with amusement from where he sat at the counter.

'You don't have to watch me, you know,' she said irritably when she couldn't figure out how many cardamom pods to use.

'You might need my help figuring out where everything is,' came his reply. She rolled her eyes and counted out five and then threw them into the pot, where her efforts were looking more like a stew than a curry.

She hoped by the time the chicken started cooking that it would be in better shape, but she was sadly disappointed. She sighed noisily, causing Daisy to look up in concern from her corner, and Dylan to leave his post at the counter to peer into the pot.

'This is your…curry?'

'It tastes better than it looks,' she said defensively, spooning up some of the sauce and offering it to him. His expression was neutral as he tasted it, and then his eyes met hers and suddenly she wasn't thinking about the sauce any more.

She'd seen scenes like this in movies before. Had wondered how feeding someone could ever really be erotic. But clearly it could be, she realised, her eyes still caught in his. Because now she wasn't thinking about Dylan tasting the sauce, but her lips.

Her skin.

Would his expression still be so neutral then? Or would he offer her something to taste in return? Like *his* lips? Like *his* skin? It would be so much better than the food she'd made that evening, and she knew that the slight kick in the sauce would have nothing on what would happen between them…

She swallowed, and her hand faltered. She cleared her throat. 'Well?'

A beat of silence passed before he answered. 'It's not bad.'

'Not...bad?'

'But it isn't curry either.'

She looked down at the pot, and then up at him again. 'Then what is it?'

'I'd say tomato stew.'

'But...but there's curry spice in it. It has a kick.'

'Well, the kick doesn't make it curry.' He narrowed his eyes. 'How many times have you made this?'

Heat immediately seared her cheeks. 'A couple.'

'Okay.' But she could see that he didn't believe her. 'Let's turn this into curry then, shall we?'

The next half an hour was distinctly different from her solo foray into curry-making. Mostly because of the way Dylan took her through the steps. It could have been a cooking show now, she thought. Or, more accurately, a one-on-one appointment with a cooking instructor.

Dylan was patient, and explained the steps to her before encouraging her to do it herself. She forced herself to ignore the thrill that went through her every time he touched her or drew closer to show her an ingredient or check how she was coming along.

But still, the time they spent fixing supper

was lovely, and settled some of the tension that had still been lingering between them since that afternoon.

'I have to say this is pretty good.'

They were sitting in the dining room adjacent to the sunroom she'd admired the day before. This room was also enclosed by glass doors, the solid wooden table clear of decoration, with only a beautiful chandelier adorning the space. Simple and tasteful, she thought, and wondered if it was the room that had her thinking that, or whether her perception of the décor had been changed by the man sitting opposite her.

'Yeah, I think we're a pretty decent team,' Dylan replied with a smile. But almost as soon as he said it his smile fell away, and Jess heard herself speaking before the tension could return.

'You're an amazing cook. And unexpectedly patient.'

He laughed, and relief went through her. 'Yeah, well, I learnt patience when I taught Anja.'

She stared at him. 'Anja's a *terrible* cook.'

'Hence the need for patience,' he said with another laugh. 'It didn't take us long to realise cooking wasn't for her, and so she was relegated to sous chef for as long as we lived together.'

The silence that followed told her he was lost in the past. And, for the life of her, Jess couldn't figure out why she wanted to help him find his way back to the present. Or at least find a way to be in the past with him.

'It sounds like you two were quite a team.'

He looked up. Smiled. 'We were. I always told her we were a well-oiled machine.' His hands stilled and Jess kept herself from asking him if he was okay again. 'Did she tell you about that?' he asked suddenly, but continued before she had the chance to reply. 'No, she wouldn't have. You told me she didn't tell you the details.'

'Do you…' she started. Faltered. Cleared her throat. Tried again. 'Do *you* want to tell me?'

His eyes met hers. 'I probably shouldn't.'

'Of course,' she said immediately, insecurity dictating the thudding of her heart.

'But I'd like to,' he continued gruffly, and she nodded, too afraid she wouldn't have a voice if she tried to speak. She waited for him to find his words, eating in silence while he did. And when he started to speak she continued, knowing it would be difficult for him to share if she was watching him.

'Anja must have told you that my father was an…absent father, long before he actually left. He went to work every morning, came back home, showered, ate, and then left for the casino. Every day, like clockwork.'

Jess's eyes strayed to Dylan's face, her hands

stilling, and she realised he was too engrossed in his story—in the emotion of it—to notice that she was watching him.

'But my mother was fine with that. She…she was able to handle that because she got to see him each day. Because some days he would return at night and sleep at home. She got to see him, and I think that was the most important for her.' He lifted his fork, ate, but Jess could see the actions were mechanical. 'And then he stopped coming home at all. I was fourteen, like I said. Anja was twelve. Both of us suspected he was gone when the routine stopped. When my mother checked out, we knew it was permanent.'

'That's…terrible, Dylan. I'm sorry.'

'I thought we already agreed we didn't have to apologise to each other for our crappy families?' he said with a wry smile. It quickly sobered. 'I remember thinking how strange it was. That even though my father barely spent time at home, not having him there at all changed…everything. We didn't used to have to worry about the house, about food, about my mother. And then—' he set his fork down, wiped his mouth with a napkin '—we had to worry about everything.' He threw the napkin aside. 'The house staff stopped coming. We had to take care of the things they used to do ourselves.' Jess saw him clench his jaw. 'And we had to take care of my mother.'

Her arms ached to comfort him, but Jess refused the urge. 'I don't understand. There was enough money. Why—?'

'Because my father had been handling all that money. He'd been running the house, paying the staff, making sure everything ran smoothly until the moment he stopped coming home. Then, everything stopped.' Dylan paused. 'Immediately after he left, I used to think the fact that he looked after us for those first fourteen years—that he hadn't used all his money on gambling—meant that he must have loved us. But then I'd remember that he *left* us, knowing that my mother didn't have access to his money, and all of the wishful thinking would disappear.' His words were so bitter, the ache in Jess's arms grew.

'Why did he leave?' Jess asked quietly, voicing the question she'd wanted to ask Anja for two years.

'I think gambling became more important to him.'

'I don't—'

'Or,' he interrupted, 'he lost control. It had been a tenuous control, anyway. Addicts...they can't indulge their addictions. If they don't get help...' He trailed off. Sighed. 'So really it wasn't about us.'

Seconds passed in silence, and again Jess resisted the urge—though it had become more pressing now—to comfort him. She told herself it was only because she understood what it was like to be abandoned. And she knew what it was like for that abandonment to be about the person who was doing the abandoning, and no one else.

Except you still think that your parents' attitude towards you has something to do with you.

Jess forced herself to speak. To distract herself from the annoying voice in her head. 'How could he keep gambling? Didn't the money ever run out?'

'The success of the family business prevented that from happening. My grandfather had made sure that my father would get a percentage of the profits every year, paid out monthly, until he died. He always had money.'

'And what about you? And Anja? And your mother?'

'My father didn't *quite* look out as well for us as his father had for him,' Dylan said with a thin smile. 'We were okay for a while after he left. My father kept cash in a safe for emergencies— that's what he told us, though now I realise it was probably for him, just in case he needed some quick cash to fund his habit—and we used that to keep us going for a while.' He picked up his fork again. 'Anja and I figured it out.'

'What happened when the money ran out?'

'I—' he cleared his throat '—I went to my father's work. I hoped I would find him there, ask him to come back.'

'But he wasn't.'

'No. Turned out his job there wasn't really that important. He was more of a...figurehead for the empire that held his name. My name,' he added. 'When I asked for him, they told me that he hadn't been there in months.'

'What did you do?'

'I asked to speak with someone who could help me.' He gave her a small smile. 'I was brazen for fourteen, but fear had forced it.' The smile faded. 'I was terrified I wouldn't be able to look after my family.'

'Oh, Dylan.' Jess reached over, laid her hand on his arm, before pulling back again.

'It worked out.' The smile was back, hiding some of the vulnerability she saw on his face. 'They sent me to the CEO. Ridge had worked closely with my grandfather, considered him a friend. He knew about my father's problems, but had no idea about what was happening with us. He made sure that we were taken care of until Anja and I got access to the trusts neither of us knew we had. My grandfather had set that up, too, though he died before we were old enough to know him.'

'How long until you got your trust?'

'Seven years.'

'So for seven years you were at this man's mercy?'

'It wasn't like that. Ridge was good to us. He taught me everything I know. Because of him, I could actually run the company my grandfather started when Ridge stepped down.'

'You've done a great job of it.'

'At what cost?'

'What do you mean?'

He shook his head, and Jess opened her mouth to press. But she stopped herself. Thought that maybe he felt as if he'd told her too much. So she didn't push. Instead, she thought about the man who had taught Dylan about his family's company.

When her stomach churned, and her memory stirred, she tried to push the thoughts away. But it was too late. Her mind kept replaying the thought. *A stranger taught Dylan about his company. Your own father wouldn't teach you about his.*

'It's been fine while you've been gone, you know,' she said suddenly. Desperately. 'They've both been fine. Anja and your mom.'

'I know. I've spoken to them. My mom—' His face tightened, his jaw clenched. 'I had her in London with me for Christmas last year.' When he lifted his eyes to hers, a pain she didn't understand shone in them. 'Anja wouldn't come.'

Why didn't she believe that that was the reason for the pain?

'She had her reasons,' Jess said instead of asking him about it. She thought about Anja's reasons for not spending Christmas with Dylan and their mother, and it took a surprising amount of strength for her not to tell him what those reasons were.

They'd done their second embryo transfer in December, and Anja had wanted to be around when they did the tests to find out whether Jess was pregnant.

It had been a stressful experience since the first transfer hadn't taken. Anja had told Jess she hadn't wanted to see her brother on top of it. Then, Jess had believed it was because Anja hadn't wanted to add to her own stress by seeing the brother who'd hurt her so badly. But now Jess wondered if it wasn't because Dylan knew Anja well enough to know that there was something on her mind, and Anja would have been forced to tell him about the baby before she was ready.

Perhaps, if things had been different, Anja

would have joined her mom and brother for a happy Christmas, and the inevitable drama of Anja's return wouldn't be hanging around their necks like an invisible noose.

But things *weren't* different, and Jess only hoped that the fact that the second transfer had taken—that there was a baby on the way— would make Anja more open to her brother's return.

And why is that so important to you? an inner voice chided her.

'Do you have siblings, Jess?' Dylan asked, interrupting her thoughts.

'No, I don't.' She forced a smile. 'I'm an only child.'

'So you don't really know how long they can hold a grudge.'

'Maybe not,' she allowed. 'But I've had one against my parents for a really long time. Does that count?'

CHAPTER NINE

'Why?'

'I've already told you they're terrible people.' She laughed, but it sounded strangled. He watched her hand go to her stomach, fingers spread over the roundness of it as though she was protecting the child she carried from her words. His heart ached. 'There's really not much more to it.'

'You keep saying that, but we both know it's a lie.' He kept his gaze on her face. 'You said you haven't seen them since you moved out.' She nodded. 'What happened?'

'What do you mean?'

'What happened to make you move out?' he clarified. 'You knew they were terrible people long before you moved out, didn't you?' Her eyes dropped from his, but she nodded again. 'So what happened to make you leave?'

He was suddenly desperate to know. Perhaps because he'd done the same thing two years ago—walked away from his family. But he'd had his reasons. His father's death had caused memories he'd ignored for years to resurface. Emotions he didn't want, didn't understand, had surged inside him.

And then he'd found out his mother had known his father had been an addict before she'd had children. She hadn't even tried to deny it when he'd confronted her. All of it had been too much for him to handle—or to keep from Anja—and so he'd left.

When guilt had nudged him, he'd tried again with his mother. He'd invited her to London, had thought they could work through it. But then, neither of them brought it up. Each day he'd told himself to, but he just…hadn't been able to. Much like he hadn't been able to walk over to Anja's house after he'd first arrived in Cape Town…

There were reasons he'd left, he thought again. So there must have been a reason Jess had left, too. He told himself he only wanted to know because he'd spilled his guts to her. But at the back of his mind he knew that wasn't true.

'What happened that made you leave, Jess?' he asked again, softly this time.

Her face went tight. 'There were…a lot of things. A lifetime of things.'

'Did they…hurt you?'

'It takes effort to hurt someone. I was no-where near that important to them.'

His eyes took in her expression, her voice, the way her shoulders had suddenly hunched. He put his hand over hers. 'Why would they have you if they didn't think you were important?'

'Because my mother fell pregnant unexpect-edly.' She paused. 'I was an...inconvenience. They didn't want me, but they didn't *not* want me either. At least not enough to do something about it.'

He stopped himself from apologising. Told himself to just listen.

'I wasn't a part of their plan. They told me that, over and over again, whenever I did some-thing they didn't approve of. Even when I did,' she added softly. 'Remember I told you about my job as a lifeguard?' He nodded. 'I applied for it at sixteen so that I could buy my new lap-top. And they *hated* it. It was at my father's country club, and they told me it made them look poor. And that looking poor wasn't a part of *their plan*. That dropping me off every day reminded them of how much it wasn't a part of *their plan*.' She stopped. 'What they actually meant was that *I* wasn't a part of their plan.'

Dylan wasn't sure what was worse. His situa-tion, where his mother had willingly had them, knowing what they'd be born into, or Jess's, where she was made to feel unwanted for most of her life.

'You know what's funny?' she interrupted his thoughts. 'I think my father actually liked the idea of an heir.' She tilted her head. 'Until I actually appeared and I was nothing like either of them. I actually *cared* about people. Heaven only knows where that came from.'

'I guess you taught yourself more than just how to cook,' he offered quietly.

'Yeah, maybe.' She smiled, and scooped the last piece of her chicken into her mouth. 'That was wonderful, thanks.'

'Dessert?' he offered spontaneously, even though he'd stopped midway through his own dinner because of their conversation. Her gaze lowered to his plate and she gave him a pointed look before shaking her head.

'I've distracted you.'

'I think we distracted each other.' He smiled at her. Made a show of eating his food. She smiled back. And his heart flipped in his chest.

Stop, an inner voice warned, even as another part of him—a stronger part—told him that he'd opened up to her for a reason. Perhaps because there was...*more* there, between them. Perhaps because he *wanted* more.

He swallowed, and began to listen to that inner voice.

'There's not much more to tell you, you know,' she said, studying him. He wondered what she saw. 'When I left university I realised it wasn't my responsibility to point due north for them any more. They were adults. So was I. And, like mature adults who didn't agree, we went our separate ways and now live separate lives.'

'They haven't tried to get in touch with you since?'

'No.' Sadness tinged her face before it was gone. 'But then, I haven't tried to contact them either. You should really finish your food,' she said, changing the subject 'It's delicious, prepared in the kitchen of one of the most revered chefs in Cape Town.'

She winked but stood, and started clearing her own dishes. Dylan might have thought it rude if it had been any other person at any other time. But he thought he understood why Jess she was doing it. She wanted to get away from him, from his questions. And, since he felt a bit raw himself, he understood.

So he finished his meal silently, and then cleared up his own dishes before joining her in the kitchen to help tidy their supper mess. The way he and Jess worked in tandem reminded him of how he and Anja had once worked. How it had been them against the world. Against their parents.

He thought about how he'd left Anja. Asked himself if that made him any better than his father. His stomach rolled with the fear of it, before it lurched with the knowledge that he *wasn't* like his father. His father hadn't needed them, but Dylan *needed* Anja. He'd discovered that when he'd been away. When he'd been plagued with how much he missed her. With how much he wanted them to be a family again, even just the two of them.

So he'd come back to try to make that happen...

But what if she didn't forgive him? What if he'd hurt her so much that, just like they'd done to their father, Anja turned her back to *him*?

The thought absolutely terrified him. Enough that he realised he couldn't afford to complicate the situation with his feelings for Jess, whatever they were. He couldn't afford to need Jess. To want her.

And so he wouldn't.

'Jess?'

'Yeah?' She was drying her hands and looked at him, and the homeliness of it sent a shot of something deep and unfamiliar through his body.

And strengthened his resolve.

'It won't happen again.'

'What won't?'

'You know, earlier…' It was strange, the heat rising up his neck. He'd faced much worse in his professional life—with his family—and yet here he was, embarrassed by a kiss.

'Oh. Oh,' she said again, her eyes wide. 'Okay.' She nodded. 'There's no hard feelings.' There was a beat of silence before she said, 'No, I didn't mean—'

'I know.' He cut her off with a slight laugh. 'Though it's a hell of a pun.'

'It was, wasn't it?' she said, chagrined. An unspoken attraction slithered over them as their eyes met again, and then she shook her head and stepped back, as if somehow it would kill it. 'Thank you for letting me stay here. I'll be out as soon as everything is fixed next door.'

'You can stay as long as you like.'

He didn't bother clarifying the implication, and she nodded and ducked her head.

But not before he saw a pretty red colour stain her cheeks.

She murmured goodnight, and left the room. Long after she had, Dylan stood in the kitchen, Daisy by his side, staring after Jess.

The next day passed in a blur of busyness.

The ceiling company had told them they would have to plaster certain sections and then repaint the entire ceiling. The good news was that they'd be able to do it all on the same day, so most of Jess's time was spent walking back and forth between Anja's and Dylan's houses, making sure the guys had everything they needed and checking on their progress.

She arranged for cleaners to come in the next day to make sure the house was one hundred per cent before she moved back in, and told herself it wasn't an excuse to spend more time with Dylan. She was *happy* about the busyness. It meant she didn't have to think about the attraction that had sunk its fangs into her the day before and wouldn't let go, no matter how much she wanted them to.

It also meant she didn't have to think about why she'd opened up to Dylan about her family. Sure, she hadn't told him everything, but she'd told him enough to make her uncomfortable. Or did she feel uncomfortable because he seemed to understand what she was telling him? That what he'd shared with her told her that he understood more than she even gave him credit for?

Unable to find answers for those questions, Jess stayed out of Dylan's way as much as she could. She answered queries about when Anja's next class would be, posted another reminder of Anja's absence on the yoga studio's social media. After a brief hesitation, she sent Anja an update on the house, and then thought it might be nice to send a picture of her baby bump as well.

It had only been two weeks since Anja had left, but Jess's belly had grown during that time and perhaps the reminder of her child would help Anja deal with her feelings about *other* members of her family.

She was trying to take the picture herself when Dylan walked in.

'I'm clearly interrupting something?'

'I'm just trying to—' She stopped the automatic answer before she told him the truth, and then gave him a smile. 'I want to take a picture of the bump for the mother and father.'

His eyebrows rose but he only said, 'Can I help you?'

'Yeah, please.'

She handed him the phone and a few seconds later she had it back with the pictures. She sent them to her laptop before shutting it. Things had suddenly become awkward and she didn't want to send the email with Dylan hovering around. It had guilt nudging her, and she realised how little she liked keeping this secret from him. But she couldn't tell him. She *wouldn't*. She had to think about Anja, and not whatever it was that had her thinking about Dylan.

'Why are you taking pictures of your stomach?' Dylan asked into the silence. 'Don't you see the parents? Your friends?'

Careful, she warned herself. 'Yes, but they're away at the moment, so I thought it might be nice to take a picture to send them.'

'How long have they been away?'

'Not too long. And they'll be back soon, too,' she added, anticipating his next question. 'They're good people, Dylan. This isn't the kind of situation that belongs in a documentary.'

She'd meant for it to be a joke, but he didn't laugh. After a while he said, 'I'm not judging your choice, Jess. Honestly, I'm not. I just can't help but wonder what happens to you after you give birth to this child.'

'I move on with my life,' she replied simply, though the question sent discomfort through her. 'It's a part of the agreement, when you do something like this.'

Though it wouldn't be for her, she thought. Not entirely. Because she'd still see the child every day when she went to work. She'd help Anja with the baby while Anja was on maternity leave, and then go back to her normal administrative duties.

That was her plan, at least. She'd taken Anja's PA job because it had seemed like the perfect opportunity to get away from her family, from their legacy. To create *her own* legacy. And while she enjoyed the organisational challenge of being a PA, it wasn't the only thing she was capable of.

She had a degree in finance. A choice that had been made when she'd still had hope her father would hire her after she'd graduated. She would be able to take over the family business one day, and finally be a part of the Steyn family. A real part. A *wanted* part. Except her father had no intention of including her, and that had been the straw that had broken the camel's back.

She told herself to snap out of thoughts of the past, but the present wasn't any better. Dylan's question had reminded her of a thought she'd shoved down a long time ago. That maybe it would be better if she didn't have to see the child she'd carried day after day. She didn't regret her decision, or think that she'd long for the child to be her own. She knew what she'd signed up for.

But she *was* worried about the things she couldn't anticipate. Like the emotion of childbirth. And the hormones that would overcome her once she saw the child who had grown inside her for nine months.

So perhaps making use of that finance degree would be a good move after she gave birth. She'd be able to give herself time to deal with the unanticipated without the emotional stress of seeing the baby every day.

But she wouldn't tell Dylan that. And she couldn't tell Anja that. But she *would* think about it.

'I appreciate your concern, Dylan. I really do.' And she meant it, she thought. 'But I know what I signed up for, and I know what it might mean for me.' She shrugged. 'I'll figure it out.'

He nodded, but his expression told her that he wanted to argue. She wouldn't let him.

'I'm going to take another look at what's happening next door.'

'No, I'll go. You were working before I got here.'

He was gone before she could protest.

CHAPTER TEN

DYLAN STAYED OUT of Jess's way for the rest of the day.

Her answers had irked him almost as much as the pull he felt towards her and was desperately trying to ignore. By the time it hit six o'clock, he was fed up with it, and decided they needed to get out of the house. Fortunately, the rain had subsided early that morning, so he made a few calls and went to find Jess.

'Hey,' he said when he found her in the sunroom. 'Not much sun to see any more.'

'You're about fifteen minutes too late. The sun's just set, and you have the perfect view of it from here.'

'I'll have to make time to see it then.'

'You never have?'

He smiled at the surprise in her voice. 'Not recently. But then, I haven't been home long. There'll be plenty of opportunities.'

'I suppose.' She paused. 'Have you come to find me because of my amazing culinary skills?'

'No,' he said, his lips slanting into a smile. 'I think we can both use a break from that tonight.'

'From my cooking? I'll try not to take offence to that.'

'From any cooking, actually,' he said, the smile turning into a grin. It was easier than he thought it would be, covering up the way his heart thudded in his chest. 'I thought we could go out.'

'Go out?' she repeated, straightening.

'Just for supper,' he added quickly. Less easy now, covering up the nerves. 'It wouldn't be a date or anything.'

'Of course not,' she said so stoically he swore she was teasing him. 'Because we're just—' She broke off with a frown. 'I was going to say friends, but I'm not sure that's what we are.'

'It's what we can be. What I'd like to be.'

But that was a lie, he thought, almost as soon as he'd said it. He didn't want to be *just* friends with her.

The realisation dislodged something in his chest he'd been ignoring since he'd met her. Since the night before, when he'd told himself he *had* to ignore it.

'Then we should seal our new friendship with a dinner out, I guess.' She smiled at him, but there was something behind the smile that told him she knew it wouldn't be that simple. 'I'm going to take a shower and then we can go. I'll see you in thirty minutes?'

'Great,' he said, and she nodded and left. A few minutes later he followed her lead, hoping that the pounding of the water against his body in the shower would give him back his ability to think logically.

Because he hadn't been. If he *had*, he wouldn't be taking her out to a restaurant. He wouldn't be entertaining their *friendship* knowing that there was something between them that could easily—*easily*—demand more.

And he couldn't have more. He'd told himself that just the day before. Had thought of all the reasons why he couldn't have more. He *knew* that he needed to focus on fixing things with Anja. On learning to forgive his mother.

Besides, there were too many complications with Jess. Too many reasons not to get attached, and risk being hurt. Too many reasons not to pursue any relationship—even a friendship— with her.

So why was he so excited to spend an evening with her?

He dressed quickly, and tried not to think about it. And then he went downstairs to wait for Jess.

His breath was swept away as soon as he saw her.

She wore a pretty blue dress that was printed with pink, yellow and green flowers over tights and boots. She'd twisted her hair up into that plaited crown again—so intricate-looking and yet so simple. He supposed the description could work for her, too. There was something so intoxicatingly intricate about her beauty, about her demeanour, and yet she wore it so casually, so easily that it seemed simple.

But he knew it wasn't. Nothing about her was.

'You look lovely.'

'Thanks,' she said with a shy smile, revealing yet another layer that wasn't simple. He'd never seen her shy before. Even when she'd been running her hands over his naked chest the first day they'd met. 'So do you, by the way.' She tilted her head. 'Maybe lovely isn't the right word.'

'Why not?'

'I don't know if your manly ego would accept it so easily,' she teased. 'So, I'm going to go with—you look very handsome tonight, Dylan.'

'Thank you,' he replied with a smile. He offered her his arm and she slid her own through it, the scent of her flowery perfume following them. He led her into the garage and opened the car door for her before sliding into his own seat and pulling out onto the driveway.

Then he took the road that would take them to the restaurant he'd only been to once before.

Ironically, it had been on a date, and he remembered being so uninterested in the woman who'd accompanied him—he'd made mistakes in the past, too—that he'd spent a decent amount of time noting the details of the restaurant décor.

But he'd so been impressed that he'd thought that one day he'd take someone he actually liked there to enjoy it with him.

'Where are we going?' Jess asked, interrupting his thoughts.

'It's a place not too far from here, actually.' He took a right, and drove the winding road up the hills that were so abundant in Cape Town.

'Are you going to tell me the name?' she asked, amusement clear in her voice.

'Buon Cibo. It's Italian for good food.'

'You're taking me to an Italian restaurant?'

'Yes.' His eyes slid over to her. 'Is that a problem?'

'No. In fact, I'm going to go out on a limb here and say that it establishes our friendship on a pretty great foundation.'

He chuckled. 'You like Italian food?'

'Love it. When I was younger…' She trailed off, and then cleared her throat and continued. 'When I was younger, my nanny was actually Italian. I'm not a hundred per cent sure where my parents found her, but I was glad they did.'

'Because of the food she made?' he asked,

hoping to make her laugh. Felt warmth spread through him when she did.

'Yes. And because she was warm and kind. Things that hadn't really been a part of my parents' MO. Anyway,' she continued after a moment, 'she used to make delicious carbonara pasta. And a delicious lasagne. And— You know what? All of her pastas were delicious.'

He smirked. 'And this was before the baby?'

She stuck her tongue out at him. 'I guess we'll see if Buon Cibo delivers on their promise.'

She stopped speaking just as he pulled in front of the restaurant, and he enjoyed the way her eyes widened. The exterior of Buon Cibo was designed to look exactly like the little cafés in Italy, except it had two large trees on either side of the door that had been decorated with small lanterns. He helped Jess out of the car, and enjoyment turned to pleasure when she saw the interior. When her reaction told him she shared his opinion of the place.

Small round tables were spread throughout the room, suited for two or four people, making it clear the place was meant for intimate dinners. Chandeliers hung from the wooden ceilings, offering light throughout the dim room, accentuated by the flickering of candles on each table.

The wall opposite the entrance was glass, and revealed that the restaurant was directly next o the ocean. Water plunged against the rocks, against the glass, in a stormy and enthralling rhythm that spoke of a passion patrons could be tempted into repeating at the end of their date.

Not that this was a date, his inner voice told him. Nor was he interested in exploring passion with Jess when he knew they would never come back from it.

He was grateful for the distraction when the maître d' showed them to their table, though he didn't know how he felt about the fact that it was right next to the thrashing waves.

'This was not what I pictured when you said we'd be going out for dinner,' Jess said as they waited for the waiter.

'You don't like it?'

'No, I love it. I just wish I'd known how…intimate it was.' Her cheeks went a riveting shade of pink. 'I would have put on something a bit more appropriate.'

'How would you dress in an…*intimate* setting like this, Jess?' His voice had gone husky at her unintentional implication.

'I…no, I didn't mean it like that.'

'I know. But it's more interesting for me to think it, anyway.' He grinned, hoping that teasing would cool the fire in his body.

'That's not how you're supposed to treat friends, Dylan.'

'I wouldn't know. My friends have never quite looked like you.'

'Stop,' she said softly. A warning, he thought, and instantly pulled back.

'We should ask about their specials, but I'd recommend the lasagne, if you're in the mood for pasta.'

'How could I not be?' she asked brightly. Gratefully, too, he knew, and mentally kicked himself for taking things too far.

'Why don't you tell me about what your life was like in the UK?' she asked once the waiter had taken their drinks order.

So he did.

He told her that the first thing he'd been struck by when he'd arrived was the cosmopolitan nature of London. It had reminded him a lot of Cape Town, and it had made him more homesick than he'd imagined he would be. He told her about the work he'd done. How he'd introduced himself to clients he hadn't yet had the opportunity to meet since taking over from Ridge.

And—though he didn't quite phrase it that way—about his obsession to bid for engineering jobs with clients who would enhance his company's reputation and portfolio. His success with those bids. How it had made him feel as if he was honouring his grandfather, the man who'd looked out for him and Anja even after his death.

How the success had made Dylan feel as if he was making up for his father's failures.

He told her how much he'd missed the warm South African weather. How he'd never quite managed to warm up even when they'd told him it was a summer's day. And, after the briefest moment of hesitation, Dylan told Jess about how much he'd missed home. And how often he'd wanted to come back.

'Why didn't you?'

'It didn't feel like the right time,' he answered. 'I...wasn't ready.'

'And you are now?'

'I don't know.' He gave her a wry smile. 'Maybe I just didn't care about the right or wrong time when I decided to come home.'

'You should tell them that. When you see them, I mean.'

'When I see Anja,' Dylan corrected automatically.

'No.' She frowned. 'When you see Anja *and* your mother.'

He opened his mouth to reply, but the waiter returned with their drinks just then and asked to take their order. Jess ordered bruschetta for her starter and went with the lasagne for her main. He ordered carpaccio and decided to have the carbonara for his main, telling her that she could have some of it if she wanted to taste.

She lifted her eyebrows. 'That's awfully kind of you, Dylan.'

'You sound surprised,' he said with a quirk of his lip.

'I'm not. Just…touched.'

He smiled at her now, and when she smiled back his heart flipped.

Get it together, Dylan.

'What were you doing before you started working for Anja?' he asked, desperate for a change of topic. One that wouldn't veer into the territory of his complicated emotions about his mother.

'Studying. I have a degree in finance.'

'Really?'

'Don't sound so surprised,' she replied, amused.

'I just…wouldn't have suspected that someone with that kind of degree would be working as a PA.'

'That's part of the reason I did it.' She fiddled with the salt shaker on the table. 'It was so different to the path I'd chosen to study, and I needed…different.'

'Why?'

The fiddling became faster. 'I studied finance because my father has an investment company. One of the largest in Cape Town.' Her fingers moved to the pepper. 'He inherited it from his father, and I thought he might want to share it with me some day.'

'But he didn't?'

'Nope.' She gave him a brave smile, but he could see the hurt. 'Apparently—' she blew out a shaky breath '—he'd been mentoring someone else at work.' Now she cleared her throat. 'To take over from him.'

'Someone who wasn't family?'

'Yes.'

'When did you find out?'

Her eyes met his. 'Just over two years ago.'

And, just like that, he got the answer to what had happened two years ago that had led her to move out. 'Did he make you believe that you'd be able to join the company some day?'

She laughed hoarsely. 'Not once.'

'Then why...' His words faded when he realised how terrible his question would sound. But she finished it for him.

'Why did I still want to? Why did I study a degree that would give me the necessary qualifications to be able to?' She dropped her hands to her lap. 'Because I wanted—' She broke off on a sigh. 'I don't know, Dylan.'

'What were you going to say?' he prodded gently. When she shook her head, he said, 'Jess, you don't have to pretend with me. Just tell me the truth.'

He held his breath during the pause after his words, and only released it when she answered him.

'I wanted to be a part of the family.' Anguish was clear in her voice, on her face. 'I thought that if I turned myself into someone that *could* be a part of the family—if I was a part of the business, if I stopped telling them where and why they were going wrong—they'd include me in their unit. It might not have been a conventional family,' she added, 'but my parents were a team. A—'

'A family that didn't include you,' he finished for her. 'Jess, I'm so—'

'Don't you dare apologise—' she interrupted him with a small smile '—I've moved on.' She paused, and Dylan thought she wasn't nearly as convincing as he suspected she wanted to be. 'And it wasn't that they wanted to exclude me entirely. My father *did* tell me I could marry the man he'd been grooming to take over.'

Dylan nearly choked on the wine he'd taken a sip of. 'He wanted you to *marry* the man? He actually said that?'

'Yeah, very seriously, too.' She rolled her eyes. 'He took my refusal just as seriously. It was clear then that what I'd wanted with my parents—what I'd hoped for—wasn't going to happen. So I moved out.'

'And you realised that what your parents did—how they acted—had nothing to do with you?' He had no idea why he'd said it, but when she looked up he knew she needed to hear it.

'It had *something* to do with me.'

'No,' he told her. 'If you believe that, then I need to believe that my father's addiction had something to do with me. That the fact that he didn't fight harder to overcome it—that he left us—had something to do with us. That my mother choosing to have us despite knowing my father had a—'

He broke off, realising what he'd said. Realising that he'd just told Jess something Anja didn't know.

Silence followed his words and, just before he could start panicking, Dylan met Jess's eyes and something passed between them that had him feeling...calmer. As if they'd reached some unspoken agreement that told him Jess wouldn't tell Anja what he'd just told her.

It was a disconcerting feeling, and he cleared his throat. 'It's not you, Jess. It's not us.'

'Do you believe that?'

'Yes,' he replied honestly. 'Coming to terms with it, on the other hand...'

Her lips curved into a half-smile and she nodded. Again, something passed between them. But this time Dylan could identify it as a kind of understanding he'd never experienced before. Not even with Anja.

He felt it draw him in, though he told himself to fight it. Reminded himself that he wasn't interested in a relationship, in a future—that thinking of either was dangerous.

He struggled with it as the waiter arrived with their starters. They were about halfway through them when he tried to distract himself. 'Do you miss them?'

'My parents?' He nodded, and she lifted her shoulders. 'I had reasons for leaving them. I *have* reasons for not keeping in touch with them. Those reasons are more important than what missing them feels like,' she said quietly. 'But I guess I do miss them.' She paused, tilted her head. 'Or maybe I just miss the parents I wish they were.'

CHAPTER ELEVEN

JESS COULD SEE that Dylan was considering what she'd just said. It was obviously something that hadn't occurred to him before. He wore the exact same expression of surprise as when he'd told her that his mother had known about his father's gambling problem before he or Anja had been born.

Since Anja had never mentioned it—and Jess was sure it was something she *would* have mentioned—Jess knew that Anja didn't know. That it was part of the reason Dylan had left.

And somehow, without words, she'd promised Dylan *she* wouldn't tell Anja either.

She told herself it was because she didn't want to get in the middle of it. Of *them*. It was the only logical explanation. Any other explanation would be anything *but* logical.

It implied that Jess didn't want to tell Anja because *Dylan* didn't want her to. Which, in turn, implied that Jess felt a certain...loyalty to

Dylan that trumped the loyalty she felt to Anja. Because if Dylan knew this and Anja didn't, it meant that he'd found out and hadn't told her. And, if that was true, Jess knew it would complicate Anja and Dylan's reunion even more.

So Jess would choose to believe that she'd agreed to keep the information to herself because she didn't want to get involved. And she would choose to believe that the guilt she felt was worth it to save Anja—and possibly the baby she carried—from the pain of a broken family.

'It's hard,' Dylan said suddenly, interrupting her thoughts. 'To face that the people who raised us weren't who we hoped they'd be.'

'Especially when they're gone and we have to face that they'll *never* be who we hoped they would be.'

He gave her a small smile, but they finished their starters in silence. Jess found herself looking at him every few minutes, and wondered if he realised how expressive his face was. Probably not, she thought, or he would have tried to hide the emotions that were clear there.

Compassion thrummed through her veins, followed closely by coldness when she realised that she shouldn't be bonding with Dylan. She shouldn't be learning the nuances of his face, of his voice. She shouldn't be understanding that he'd left because he'd been in pain.

Because leaving had caused *Anja* pain. Anja, her best friend. The only person in her life who actually seemed to deserve Jess's love. Who'd made Jess feel loved. Dylan was not her friend. No, he was the man who'd broken a piece of her best friend's heart. He was her best friend's *brother*.

So what if he seemed to understand her? If it seemed they had a lot in common? He was off-limits. And she couldn't—*wouldn't*—consider the dangerous emotions that were suddenly whirling around inside her.

Instead, she said the only thing that she could: Dylan needed to open up to someone else.

'You need to talk to someone about your father's death.'

'Excuse me?'

'You heard me. You need to talk through your feelings about your father's death, about him leaving. About—' she hesitated '—about your mother.' Left it at that.

'You mean…like a therapist?'

'That's not a bad idea, but it's not what I meant.' She let the words linger. 'I meant a… friend.'

Seconds passed before he said, 'I don't have that many friends.'

'You have Anja,' she told him. 'And your mother. No,' she said over his protest. 'I don't know the details of what happened with your mother, but if it can be salvaged, salvage it.'

'I...don't think that's going to happen.'

'Dylan—'

But the arrival of their main courses interrupted what she was going to say, and the turmoil on Dylan's face prompted her not to continue when the waiter left. Instead, Jess dug into her meal with a gusto she'd only experienced as a pregnant woman.

'Do you want some of mine?' Dylan asked, the turmoil now replaced with faint humour. It made him look softer, more handsome.

No, Jess!

'Yeah, thanks.' She took a forkful of spaghetti, but paused before she brought it over to her mouth. 'What's funny?'

'What do you mean?' he asked with an innocent expression that immediately had her narrowing her eyes.

'Are you *laughing* at my eating habits?'

'No.' But he laughed aloud now, and her eyes narrowed even further. 'I told you I was ordering this so you could taste it.'

'But then you looked at me like you thought I *needed* to taste it.'

'I did *not*.'

'You better not be lying to me.'

He chuckled. 'I'm not. Now, do you want to

taste the pasta, or are you going to spend the rest of the night arguing with me?'

'I want to taste the pasta,' she grumbled, but winked at him.

The rest of the evening wasn't as tense as the first part, though the ghost of it hovered over them for the rest of the night. But, since neither of them brought it up, the conversation was light, happy, as though they hadn't spoken about their pasts that night.

It was late when they finished and as they walked out of the restaurant Jess paused to turn back. 'This was a really lovely evening at a really lovely place.'

'I'm glad you liked it,' he replied, standing next to her. 'Jess…'

Something about his voice had her turning towards him, and she sucked in her breath when she saw his expression.

'I know that this is probably the last thing that we should do after everything that's happened— after everything we've said—today,' he whispered, closing the distance between them and lifting a hand to her cheek. 'But I'm going to anyway.'

She opened her mouth to reply, but his lips were on hers before she could. It tasted sweet, a mixture of dessert and coffee. But beneath it Jess could also taste the man. That pure masculine taste that she'd only really experienced once before.

With him.

This time, though, the kiss wasn't as desperately heady as the one they'd shared in the forest. This kiss was soft and deliberate, a gentle sigh that had her heart racing. She felt the heat of his hand on her face as his other hand settled gently on her waist, a slow burn that went from the point of contact straight to her blood, warming her body as leisurely as a bath would.

With bubbles, too, she thought foolishly when he deepened the kiss—still tender, still cautious—and it felt as if there were bubbles in her stomach, on her skin. She gave a soft moan and pressed closer, her own hand sliding up from where it had rested on his chest to cup his cheek. His beard prickled, aroused, and it was strange that the feeling was more jarring through the contact of her hand than against her face.

She was breathing heavily when she pulled back, and she felt a flip in her stomach that had nothing to do with the way Dylan had made her feel. The hand on his face immediately lowered to the movement and, smiling, she looked up at him.

She wasn't sure what she'd expected. But it wasn't the following of his hand to where she'd put hers. It wasn't the reverent look on his face as he felt the slight pressure of the baby moving inside her.

It reminded her that he wouldn't be nearly as touched when he found out whose baby she was carrying. It told her that she was playing both sides. That she was betraying Anja with whatever was happening between her and Dylan. That she had betrayed Dylan by getting involved with him—even though it had been unintentional—when she was connected so deeply to his sister.

Tension crept into her body and settled in the muscles of her shoulders, her neck. She stepped back, away from him, and then walked to the car, waited for him to unlock it so she could get in. She didn't give him a chance to open the door for her this time—didn't give *herself* a chance to deal with the confusion on his face. She only shook her head when he said her name, and told herself to breathe when the tension inside her spread between them.

The ride back home was short, quiet, and Jess was almost relieved when they pulled into the driveway of Dylan's house.

Almost.

Except there was already a car in front of the house when they got there, and Jess inhaled sharply when she recognised it. She let the breath out in a shudder just as Dylan said, 'Anja's home.'

CHAPTER TWELVE

THERE WAS A sick feeling in Dylan's stomach.

To be fair, he couldn't blame it entirely on returning from dinner with his sister's best friend to find said sister on his doorstep. No, the feeling had started the moment he'd felt the baby Jess was carrying moving against his hand. When he'd seen her face and worried that the wonder and amazement he saw there—that the wonder and amazement *he'd* felt—would turn into heartbreak when she gave that baby away.

The feeling had settled when Jess had walked away from him, breaking the warmth of their kiss and their connection that had grown during their dinner. And when he'd tried to do something about it and he'd got the cold shoulder, the silent treatment on the way home.

But now he was home, and his sister was back, and there would be no more time to think of it.

He pulled the car into the garage and then

got out slowly. He heard Jess behind him as he walked to the front of his house where his sister was and, by the time he got there, Anja was standing outside, Chet next to her.

Dylan's eyes first went to their hands—to the tight hold he could see between them. And then he looked at his sister. Really looked. And really saw, for the first time in years. She'd got skinnier. And her face was tougher, its lines creased into a tight expression that told him she wasn't going to take it easy on him. But other than that she looked the same, and the emotion that clogged his throat had him wanting to walk right to her and pull her into his arms.

Instead, he shoved his hands into his pockets. 'It's good to see you, sis.'

'It's a…surprise to see you, Dylan.' Her voice was hoarse and she cleared her throat. 'How long have you been back?'

'Just over a week.'

'And you didn't tell us? Me or Mom?'

'I wanted it to be a surprise,' he said lamely, and belatedly thought that maybe it *was* lame. That maybe his plan to come home and reconcile with his sister was just plain *lame*.

'Well, it's certainly been that.'

Silence spread between them, and then Anja's eyes shifted to behind him and her stormy expression cleared. 'Jess!'

His sister stalked past him as if he wasn't even there and enveloped Jess in a hug. Jealousy beat an uncomfortable rhythm in his blood and all he could do was stand there as Chet walked past him, too, thumped him on the back in greeting and went over to hug Jess.

'Your stomach has grown so much!' Anja said and lowered to her haunches. Jess's eyes fluttered over to him, and something crossed her face that he couldn't quite read.

'Yeah. But it's only been two weeks, An.'

'Much too long for my liking,' Anja murmured to Jess's belly and Dylan's stomach dropped slowly, steadily, his mind still trying to comprehend what his eyes were telling him.

Anja straightened and turned to Dylan. 'Did Jess tell you?'

'Tell me what?'

'You asked me not to,' Jess interrupted, and her eyes went from Anja's to Dylan's. This time he could clearly see the apology on her face.

'So he doesn't know?' Anja asked, but the question wasn't directed at Jess. It was directed at him. Which made absolutely no sense. How was he supposed to know what he didn't know?

'I don't know what you're talking about.'

'Maybe we should take this conversation inside?' Jess interrupted.

'What conversation?' Dylan demanded, his

heart thudding from the tension. 'Someone just tell me what you're talking about. Now,' he snapped, when Jess opened her mouth again.

'Relax,' Anja told him. 'This isn't Jess's fault. She's right. I asked her not to tell you.' She shifted closer to Chet and took his hand. 'Jess is carrying our baby, Dylan. Chet and I are going to be parents.'

And immediately Dylan knew why his stomach had dropped earlier. Why he suddenly recognised it as sick anticipation. It didn't matter that it made no sense—how could he have anticipated the news Anja had just told him? How could he have known that Jess was carrying his sister's child? *His* niece or nephew?

But all he knew for sure was that the feeling was there, and it made him feel foolish.

Just like trusting Jess did.

'Why?' he asked hoarsely. 'When?'

'We should go inside,' Jess said again. Dylan nodded, but he didn't look at her. Couldn't. Not even when she said, 'No, actually, you all should go inside. You need to talk about this and…' Her voice faded, though Dylan sensed everyone knew what she was referring to. Him. His return. Why he'd left. 'I don't need to be there.'

'You can be,' Anja said softly. 'You're as much a part of the family as any of us are.'

'No,' Dylan heard himself say. 'She's not. And she's right, this should be between all of us.'

'Dylan—'

'No, Anja, he's right,' Jess said. 'I'll be next door.'

'I thought you said the ceiling wouldn't be done until tomorrow?'

'They finished the painting today. I'll open all the windows and be upstairs. The smell shouldn't be as bad there.'

And then she was gone, leaving Dylan alone with his sister and brother-in-law.

It was silly to cry. Jess knew it, and yet she still felt the tears slip down her cheeks.

She could blame it on the hormones. And they probably deserved some of the blame. But most of it came from the look on Dylan's face after he'd discovered that she was carrying Anja and Chet's baby.

And the vicious reminder that she wasn't a part of their family.

Her breath shuddered out as she opened the windows of Anja's house, the fresh, brisk autumn air relieving the smell of paint in the house. It was better upstairs, as she'd thought it would be, and after she opened the windows her eyes fell on the chair that still sat in front of one of them.

Had it only been a week ago that she'd seen Dylan for the first time? It didn't seem right that she could feel his disappointment in her—his hurt *because* of her—so profoundly when she'd only known him for such a short span of time. And yet there she was, wiping tears from her eyes because of it, and trying to figure out what to do next.

She couldn't stay in Dylan's house any more. She suspected that she'd burnt that bridge, well and truly, though it hadn't been *entirely* her fault. Perhaps if Anja and Dylan's relationship hadn't been so damaged, things wouldn't seem so bad for him. Except that it *was* damaged, and Jess was carrying the reminder of the extent of it.

She knew now that every time Dylan looked at her he'd be reminded. Added to the fact that he'd been acting so strangely about her surrogacy even before he'd known who she was a surrogate for.

So she couldn't stay at Dylan's, and Anja's was out of the question with the smell of paint still lingering in the air. She could find a hotel—there was no way she'd find anything cheap at such short notice—but that would take from her savings. Savings she'd need after she'd given birth and needed to separate herself from Anja and Dylan.

It was clear that would be her only option

now. Her friend would put up a fight, Jess knew, but Jess needed space. Away from the baby, and away from their uncle. Though she knew that wasn't the only reason.

She'd become comfortable with her life, just as she had been before she'd started working with Anja. Was it perfect? No, but she hadn't expected it to be. And perhaps that was why she'd lingered, avoiding what she'd needed to do, just as she had with her parents.

But she needed her independence. She saw that now so clearly that she wasn't sure why she hadn't before. She needed to stop relying on people she *thought* were family, and she needed to start relying on herself.

So she would drive to a hotel and spend the night there. And soon she'd move into her own flat. She'd save as much as she could while she still worked for Anja, but she'd start making plans. She *would* survive this. She'd survived worse.

Jess sighed and sank into the couch, her body aching from the strain of being pregnant and the tension of the day. The brisk breeze still drifted through the air and she pulled a throw over herself. She switched on the television, and waited for Anja to tell her their discussion was over.

She would pack up her things and go to a hotel, she thought, even as her eyelids started to close…

* * *

Dylan found Jess wrapped in a fleece throw in front of the television. It took him a moment to realise that she was sleeping, and seeing her like that wiped away all the righteous indignation he'd felt from the moment he'd offered to tell her she could come back to his house.

Instead, he settled on the opposite couch, his body and soul weary from the last couple of hours. He could do with a break from the tension between him and his sister. That was the only way he could describe what had transpired between them. He was exhausted, and the space he wanted so that he could figure out how he felt about everything was unavailable as Anja and Chet were sleeping over.

He had plenty of spare rooms—the house had been designed that way because he'd hoped one day to have a big family. To have his and his sister's kids playing around, having sleepovers. He wasn't sure that would happen any more. Which made sense considering that his sister hadn't even told him she was expecting a child.

Could he even call it that? he thought, rubbing a hand over his face. He immediately felt bad about it, and let out a shaky breath. It was all too much for him—Jess, the surrogacy, seeing his sister again.

Finding out his sister had had a miscarriage

and how she'd struggled with it afterwards. Finding out Jess had offered to help them have a child when Anja had been so close to giving up. The unselfish reasons Jess had described to him when she'd told him about the surrogacy were so much more profound now. So was his fear for her when she had to give the child away, though heaven only knew why.

She was carrying his niece or nephew and *she hadn't told him.*

Did it matter that Anja had asked her not to? Maybe. But it still felt like a betrayal, that she'd broken his trust. Which was ridiculous, considering that he hadn't even known her long enough to trust her.

Logically, he knew that. But, just like he'd thought before, nothing about the situation with Jess felt logical. It hadn't been logic that had softened, warmed in his chest when she'd shown him her sympathy and told him he needed to talk about his problems. It hadn't been reason that had pushed him into kissing her. There was something more there that had nothing to do with logic, and it terrified him.

And maybe that was why he felt the way he did.

Or maybe it was all a distraction to keep him from thinking about how coldly his sister had greeted him. Or how stilted their interactions had been. They hadn't spoken about anything other than the baby since Anja had told him she was too tiredfor anything else.

He couldn't argue, considering she'd travelled eighteen hours to get home. But he knew it wasn't the travelling that had tired her. It was the first of many difficult conversations they were going to have.

It was going to be a process, he thought. One he couldn't speed up merely because he wanted to. He needed to give Anja time to process. Hell, he needed to give himself time to wade through all his thoughts, all his feelings. About his family, yes. But also about the woman who whimpered so softly in her sleep.

So he stayed in Anja's house for a while longer and, when he was ready, did what he'd offered to do. He closed all the windows and then lifted Jess into his arms and carried her to the house next door.

CHAPTER THIRTEEN

WHEN SHE WOKE UP, Jess wasn't entirely sure where she was.

It took her a while to figure out that she was in a bed. And that that bed was the one she'd slept in for the second time now...in Dylan's house.

So much for getting a hotel room, she thought. And then realised that being there meant someone had *brought* her there the night before.

She didn't want to spend too much time thinking about who.

Because though she knew Chet could easily have carried her the short distance to Dylan's house, he would have more likely woken her. Which left only one other option...

Pushing away fanciful thoughts of how sweet, how romantic it must have been, Jess got out of bed and had a shower. She hadn't brought another set of clothes with her, so she pulled on the tights from the night before—ignoring the way her heart sank at the memory of how different things had been when she'd worn them then— and her woollen oversized jersey with boots. It wasn't entirely new, but she hadn't worn this combination before.

Besides, who was she trying to impress? Certainly not the friends who'd seen her with her legs in the air while she'd been impregnated with their child. And *certainly* not the man who'd brushed her off so completely the day before.

With that in mind, she pulled her hair into a bun at the top of her head and began packing. Fifteen minutes later, she walked with her suitcase to the kitchen. She was surprised to find no one there, but she heard the deep rumble of male voices from the dining room. Leaving her suitcase in the kitchen passageway, she made her way there.

It was strange seeing Dylan and Chet there, talking as though there hadn't been a boulder of tension that had descended on them the day before. They stopped when she walked in. Chet smiled at her, but Dylan's face immediately soured before settling into a blank expression. She nearly rolled her eyes.

'I'm not sure how I ended up in bed here last night, but I'm willing to bet it was one of you.'

'Hey, you *are* carrying my child,' Chet replied with a wink, and she felt her mouth curve.

'Though, let's be honest, that wouldn't have kept you from waking me up and telling me to walk back to the house.' Her eyes went to Dylan and she felt the amusement waver. 'Thank you.'

'No need,' he replied smoothly.

She clenched her jaw. 'Well, I think there is, so I'm saying thanks. Also for letting me stay here while everything was happening next door.'

'You're welcome.' His eyebrow quirked. 'Better?'

'Much,' she replied, and then turned her attention to Chet. 'Where's Anja?'

'She went for a run. Said she'd see you when she gets back.'

'Well, she can see me next door. I'm going to head over, make sure everything's okay before the cleaners arrive in an hour.'

'You don't want breakfast first?' Chet asked.

'I'll make myself something at your place.'

'You sure about that?' Dylan interjected now.

'Why wouldn't I be?'

'Just because I've tasted your cooking and...' He let the words drift and annoyance stirred. Which was strange, since she was fairly certain that she would have been amused if it hadn't come from him.

'And yet I've survived for twenty-six years,' she said wryly. 'I'll see you next door, Chet. And…' she hesitated '… I guess I'll see you around, Dylan.'

She pretended that she hadn't seen the questioning look Chet sent her and picked up her bag, giving Daisy a head pat before she left.

It felt strangely as if she was turning over a new page. And perhaps she was, she thought, considering the plans she'd made the night before. Granted, it hadn't worked out for her to sleep at a hotel the previous night, but perhaps that was a blessing in disguise. Now she could keep that money in her savings.

When she got to Anja's place she made herself something to eat, ignoring the way her stomach wished she'd taken up Chet's offer to have breakfast next door. She could have had bacon and eggs instead, and tried to make up for the lack of it by making her single cup of tea for the day.

She was curled up on the couch when Anja walked in.

'Glad to see you're having a good balanced breakfast,' Anja said, flopping down on the couch opposite Jess. Her hair was still wet from her morning shower, the curls piled up on top of her head, much like Jess's.

'Eating for two and all that,' she said, tilting

her bowl of oats for Anja to see. 'You can't have had breakfast yet?'

'I haven't, and I'm starving.'

'Why didn't you eat something before you came over?'

'Because it would entail spending more time with my brother?'

Jess's heart thudded at the mention of Dylan. 'Well, you *did* come back to do that…didn't you?'

'I guess. I don't know. I'm just so…*mad*.'

Jess bit back the *why?* on the tip of her tongue and nodded. 'You should tell him that.'

'I don't think it would go down particularly well,' Anja replied dryly.

'Actually, I think it might. He doesn't know why you're mad, Anja, besides the obvious reason. And it's about time you stop carrying it around with you, too.'

Anja narrowed her eyes. 'Since when do you push for family reconciliations?'

She choked out a laugh. 'Since you came back from Sydney as soon as you heard he was back?' A beat of silence passed. 'You can't tell me that you finished everything you wanted to?'

'We finished the last of the work on the studio. I'd hoped to do more…but I wanted to be here. The rest we can do via email or video chat.' Anja sighed. 'I guess you're right.'

'As usual,' Jess teased.

'Ha ha.'

Jess let Anja mull it over and finished her breakfast. She made some coffee for Anja and handed it over. Anja murmured her thanks, adding, 'How do you know? That Dylan doesn't know why I'm mad, I mean?'

She should have worn her hair down, she thought, when she felt the tell-tale heat of a blush start in her cheeks. 'We talked over the last few days.'

'About me?'

'About him, mostly.'

'And?'

Jess struggled to find an answer that didn't make her feel as if she was betraying Dylan's trust. 'He's come back to make things right. I know,' she said when Anja opened her mouth. 'I know that things are messy and painful between you two. But he's come back, and so did you. For the sake of your child, his niece or nephew, and for *your* sake, you should at least try to talk to him about it.'

Anja rolled her eyes. Then threaded her fingers together. 'Low blow, Steyn.'

'I know,' she said sympathetically. 'But it wouldn't hurt if it wasn't true.'

They sat in silence after those words, and then Anja said, 'He *did* take time off work to be home. He hasn't since—'

'Since he left.'

'Since long before then, actually.' Anja gave her a strange look. 'Are you…is there something going on between you two?'

'What?' There was no stopping the blush now. 'No, of course not. Why would you say that?'

'Because my brother doesn't just share how he feels with people. Hell, I lived with him for almost two decades and I still don't know some of the things he felt then. That's part of the problem.'

'I was just there at the right time, I guess.'

'Maybe.' But Anja looked worried. 'You're not interested in him?'

'No,' she said immediately. *Not any more, anyway.* 'I was civil with him because of you. And this baby.' She didn't have to mention the kisses. 'I know it would be much too complicated, Anja.'

'It would be,' her friend agreed.

'Good thing there's nothing to worry about then, isn't it?' Jess replied, and ignored the sick feeling in her chest at the lie.

Because she *was* worried. She was *very* worried.

* * *

Dylan saw her as soon as he got there, and was about to turn back—coward that he was—when she turned and saw him.

'Oh,' she said softly. 'I'll leave.'

'No, you don't have to,' he replied immediately. Though he was still mad at her, Dylan hated that the easiness between them had been replaced by...by whatever was happening now. A mixture of tension and apology. Of words unspoken and words that had been said. 'I'll leave.'

'No, this is your place.'

She turned, and he could almost see her eyes taking in the magnificent view from the hilltop he'd taken her to a few days ago.

His place of comfort.

Where he'd opened up to Jess.

Where he'd kissed her.

He pushed away the memories when she turned back. 'You shouldn't have to leave just because I'm here.'

'I'm not,' he said in a short tone that proved exactly the opposite of what he'd said. 'I just wanted to be alone.'

'So I'll go.' She walked past him.

The words were out of his mouth before he could help it. 'Why were you here?'

The crackling of leaves and sticks under her feet went quiet. 'I wanted to think.'

'About?'

She gave a small laugh. 'Why don't you take a guess?'

He didn't reply. Couldn't, when what he would guess sounded incredibly self-centred. There was no way she was thinking about him. Even if *she* was part of the reason he'd needed time outside, to think alone.

After a moment he heard the crunching of leaves again, and he whirled around. 'Jess.'

She stopped, turned back to look at him. 'Yeah?'

'Anja and I...we had a conversation this morning.' It had been one of those conversations that had picked his emotions apart and left them out to dry. Naked. Raw. 'She told me you told her to give me a chance.'

She shook her head. 'I told her she needed to start thinking about her child.'

'The child you're carrying.' As if he could forget.

'Yes,' she told him. 'I see your opinion hasn't changed despite the fact that you now know I'm carrying your niece or nephew.'

'I have no opinion on this.'

'You and I both know that's not true.'

'Your agreement with my sister has nothing to do with me.'

He watched her face tighten.

'I'll remember that the next time I have to talk her into having a conversation with you.'

'So you *did* tell her that.'

'For her child's sake.'

'And yet she made it sound like it was for the sake of this family, too.'

'What do you want from me, Dylan?' she asked in an exasperated tone.

'The truth,' he growled.

'Fine. I told her to give you a chance. For the child's sake, for hers, and yes, for you, too.' The admission cost her, he thought, taking in the expression on her face. 'I care about... I care,' she finished, and lifted a hand to brush at her face.

'Why?' he asked, caught by her now. Anger had flushed her cheeks, making the golden brown of her skin almost luminous. 'Why do you care?'

'I'm asking myself that very question right now.'

'And what answer have you come up with?'

His back was turned to the view he'd returned to for solace, the beauty in front of him now much more appealing. He shouldn't have noticed what a lovely picture she made. Standing in the woods, tall, dark trees around her, dull brown leaves at her feet. She looked like a woodland creature, though he couldn't blame it on the plaid shirt and jeans she wore.

He *did* blame it on the way she carried herself. The ease, the natural rhythm of her. Even when she was standing there, looking at him in annoyance, she looked as if she belonged there. As if her selflessness, her kindness, belonged in a natural setting.

'That I'm crazy.'

'You're not crazy.' If *she* was, then so was he.

But then, maybe that was the answer.

'No? Then how do you explain what's been happening over the last few days? Because you might not have known just how off-limits I was, Dylan, but *I* did. I knew the moment I found out the sexy guy living next door was my best friend's brother, the uncle of the child I carried. I *knew* that I shouldn't have got involved with you.'

She threaded her fingers together, as though she didn't know what to do with her hands. 'And yet, when you brought me here, when you told me all of those things about your family... I felt... I don't know, *attracted* to you.' She said the word with a disgust he struggled not to feel offended by. 'And, you know, because of all that—' she waved a hand at his body, and amusement coloured the insult '—and so I kissed you. And I went on a date with you. And none of that nonsense about us being friends,' she added, 'because we both know that wasn't a friendship date.'

He didn't know what to say. But he'd asked for it, he knew. He'd pushed her, and he couldn't be upset that she was giving him the information he needed. That he wanted.

The only problem was that nothing she was telling him turned off whatever it was that he felt whenever he saw her. It didn't matter how angry—or how raw—he was, his heart ached and his stomach flipped every single time he saw her.

'You know what the worst part is?' she asked. 'That I got in the middle of whatever's going on with you and Anja. I *ran* right in the middle of your family drama while running away from my own.'

'You've helped,' he said softly.

'Have I?' She lifted her brows. 'When you came here, your question was more accusation than gratitude.'

'I'm…sorry about that.' The apology was a surprise. As was the sincerity he felt as he said it. 'The conversation with Anja… It was tough, and I came out here to deal with…everything.' He shrugged, wishing the pain was as easy to shake as the words. 'I'm glad you asked her to talk with me.'

'She wanted to,' she replied after a moment. 'She just needed a shove in the right direction.'

He almost smiled. 'Thank you.'

'Sure.' Silence pulsed between them, and then she said, 'I'm going to leave before we get into another argument that tempts me into shoving more literally.'

He nodded. Told himself what he wanted to ask her wouldn't be worth the turmoil her answer would no doubt bring. And then he asked it anyway. 'Why didn't you tell me, Jess?'

'Anja asked me not to.'

'And it was just that simple for you?' Anger stirred, and then burrowed into him. 'It was just that simple to keep something I should have known from me?'

'Yes,' she replied quickly, and then exhaled sharply. 'That's what you want me to say, isn't it? That it was simple for me to keep this secret from you?'

'I just want the truth.'

'No, you don't, Dylan. You want another reason to be angry with me.'

Disbelief made him splutter his words out. 'You think I *want* to be angry with you?'

'Yes, I do,' she replied. 'Because it would be easier to be angry with *me* than with your mother. With your father. With…' she hesitated '…with yourself.'

'No,' he denied. 'I *trusted* you, Jess. You broke—' his voice went hoarse '—you broke my trust.'

'Because I was being loyal to the only person who's ever been loyal to me?' she demanded. 'Because I was keeping *Anja's* trust?' She shook her head. 'She's like family to me, Dylan. She *is* my family. And you know why that's so important to me.' She paused. 'Whatever you and I shared these past few days—' She broke off and he nearly protested, desperate to hear what she was going to say.

Instead, silence followed her words before she blew out a breath. 'It wasn't easy,' she told him. 'It wasn't simple. But Anja trusted me, too. And—' Jess lifted her shoulders '—being able to trust your family, knowing that they'll be there for you, that they'll do what's right for you, even when it's hard for them? That's what family's supposed to do.'

She stopped speaking then, her eyes studying his face, telling him that she had more to say. He wasn't wrong.

'That's why you're really upset, Dylan. Because your parents broke your trust. They left. Even though your mother was still there,' she continued, 'she wasn't *there*. Not in the way you needed her to be. And I'm sure…what you found out about her made that feel even worse.'

Dylan felt the agreement inside him—felt the truth of it—but he didn't speak.

'You're angry at her because of it. And at your father, for all the horrible things he put you through. But you're also angry at yourself. For leaving,' she said when he looked at her, and he wondered how she knew things he hadn't even admitted to himself. 'So if you need to deal with that by being angry with me, go right ahead. But realising it and facing the anger you have is going to help you fix what's wrong with you and Anja.'

She left then, but he didn't follow. He needed time to think, especially since Jess had just added to the list of things he needed to think about, easily summarising feelings he'd struggled to figure out for the longest time in just a few minutes. By the time he made his way back to the house, Dylan knew just how right Jess had been.

And damn if that didn't complicate things.

CHAPTER FOURTEEN

DAYS LATER, ANJA told Jess that she, Chet and Dylan were taking a trip to the coastal town of Langebaan to see their mother. The news was unexpected, as was her insistence that Jess go with them.

'No,' Jess said, feeling ambushed. She was still staying in Anja's house, working, thankfully, which helped her keep her mind off Dylan and the inner voice telling her it was time to move on. She'd avoided Dylan as much as she could, which was possible since Anja mostly went over to his house after work. She stayed there for hours and when she came back looked exhausted and emotional. They were sorting it out, Chet had told Jess one night, since he was her only companion for the time Anja was away. And sorting it out was a process, Anja had told her the following day at work. It hadn't been easy since their issues extended far beyond what either of them had known, but they were working through it. And now the final step was to speak to their mother.

Jess's efforts to avoid Dylan were now in vain since he stood on the other side of Anja's lounge, leaning against the wall with his arms crossed. She suspected he was going for a nonchalant look, but he only succeeded in looking broody and sexy and Jess cursed the pregnancy hormones for making her notice.

'You don't need me there,' she said, looking from Anja to Chet. She studiously avoided Dylan. 'I'm just going to be in the way.'

'No, you won't be,' Anja told her. 'My mom wants to see you again. And, you know, the baby,' she said, which was a real punch in the gut for Jess. How could she say no?

Her eyes flickered to Dylan, and then back at Anja again.

Oh, yes, *that* was how.

'It won't be comfortable for me to sit in the back of your car,' Jess protested, clutching at straws now. 'Either of yours,' she added, looking at Chet.

Both of them had trendy little cars that were incredibly impractical for a pregnant woman—and for a family. Anja was planning to trade in her car before the baby was born, but there was no way she'd be able to do it before this impromptu little trip.

'We've already thought about that,' Anja said, her enthusiasm a stark contrast to the fatigue she'd shown over the last few days. Jess could feel her resistance weakening. 'Dylan will drive up in his car. He's agreed for you to drive with him.'

'Has he now?' she asked, and cocked an eyebrow at Dylan. He gave her a smile that made her want to punch it from his sexy mouth.

'Yeah, and he has more than enough space. Besides, Jess,' Anja continued, her voice softening. 'None of us want to leave you here alone.'

And, with that, her resistance broke all together. 'Fine, but don't think I don't know you were working me.'

'I was *not*,' Anja said in mock insult. 'If I was—and, I repeat, I was not—I would have mentioned how much we consider you to be a part of our family, and that any family trip would be incomplete without you.'

With a laugh, she ducked out of the way of the cushion Jess threw at her.

Though she'd been joking, Anja's words had stayed with Jess in the days before they took the ninety-minute drive to Langebaan, a tiny town on the West Coast of South Africa. It had made Jess realise how much she wanted Anja's words to be true. And that had made her wonder—or panic—about whether she'd offered to be Anja's surrogate because she so desperately wanted to be a part of that family.

Of any family.

At the time, it hadn't even occurred to Jess. She'd only offered because she'd wanted to help, and it had been a real, tangible way for her to do so. She loved Anja—more than the employer she was, or the friend she'd become. She loved Anja... Well, Jess imagined she loved Anja like she would a sister...

Except she'd never had a sister—or any sibling—so how could she possibly know?

Now she worried that she'd become Anja's surrogate because she'd wanted to protect that love. *Her* love. *Her* feelings. Because surely Anja couldn't turn her back on Jess when Jess had carried her child? She couldn't stop caring about Jess, or toss her away like Jess's parents had...

Unless she could.

Because Jess would have served her purpose then, wouldn't she? She would have done what she'd offered to do, and given Anja the child she'd always wanted. What would keep Anja from turning from Jess then? What would keep that bond she thought she shared with her friend from crumbling?

Jess had already learnt that she didn't have

much purpose in her life. The degree she'd worked so hard towards was useless. No matter how hard she'd tried, her parents didn't want her. And if she didn't have a purpose—if she was useless—why would Anja want to keep her around?

Jess sucked in her breath. Told herself not to cry.

But the tears came anyway.

'I know this might not be exactly how you would have liked to travel,' Dylan said wryly. 'But we could at least try for some civility.'

He felt Jess shift beside him, but kept his eyes on the road. It was bad enough that he was stuck in such a confined space with her. He wouldn't look at her, too, and have that sexy and sweet look she had going for her distract him even more.

He'd been annoyed when his sister had told him about the plan. Partly because he'd had to put Daisy in a doggy hotel while they were away. Partly because he'd had to leave his house and he'd just grown comfortable living there again.

But mostly it was because he really didn't want to speak to his mother about the past. But as soon as Anja had found out that their mother had known about their father's gambling problem before they'd been born, she'd been determined to find out why their mother had decided to have them.

Though that determination had only come after the shock, the tears, the hurt, he thought. And knew that they were only in store for more of the same.

But they'd been making progress, and for the first time he'd been able to articulate why he'd left. Because he'd felt as if their mother had betrayed them. Broken their trust. Because she'd abandoned them by reacting the way that she had to their father's abandonment, even though she'd *known* what she'd signed up for.

Because he hadn't wanted to add the pain of knowing all that—pain he knew the extent of—to Anja's grief. Because he hadn't been able to deal with his own grief over a man who hadn't deserved it.

He hadn't mentioned his fear that maybe *he'd* abandoned Anja just like their parents had. Didn't want to in case Anja didn't feel that way, and he'd put it in her mind. No, he'd rather keep that to himself. And, even without disclosing it, Dylan felt…hopeful. Hopeful that maybe their family could move past the hurt, the abandonment, the betrayal.

And perhaps that was why he'd agreed to take the trip. For the sake of closure. And as for taking Jess along…what was he supposed to do? Say no? That would have for sure sounded his sister's alarms, and he knew that she already had her suspicions about his relationship with Jess. He suspected the only reason she hadn't asked him about it was because she'd had the conversation with Jess, and she'd chosen to trust her friend's word on it.

Good thing, too, or the progress he and Anja had made might have been wiped away.

'I'm sorry,' Jess replied, interrupting his thoughts. 'I didn't realise civility required words.'

'Well, we have over an hour left of this trip, so if you're happy with being quiet for the rest—'

'I am,' she said quickly, and he frowned.

They weren't on the best terms, he knew, but this withdrawn, sullen person wasn't the Jess he'd got to know. She wasn't even the one he'd fought with that night that felt like so long ago, or the one he'd had the terse but somehow productive conversation with in the woods.

'Are you okay?' he asked.

'I thought we were going to be quiet?'

'And if I thought that you wanted to be quiet because you were annoyed with me, I would have been. Except that isn't the case.'

'You're an expert in my emotions now?'

'No, but I'm a good businessman and that requires being able to read people.' He glanced over, and then looked back at the road. 'It helps that I *do* know you.'

'I think you're overestimating your knowledge,' she said, but he could sense her resistance was waning.

'Or underestimating it,' he replied quietly. 'What's wrong?'

He saw her shake her head and then bite her lip. He didn't push, didn't say anything else since he understood her hesitation. Understood that he was responsible for it. They'd been put in a hell of a situation, he knew, but his behaviour hadn't helped.

He'd overreacted. Or he'd just reacted, he thought, to his trust being broken while he was still trying to deal with his mother breaking his trust. While he was still trying to deal with all the other things Jess had pointed out to him.

So he needed to apologise for taking it all out on her. And perhaps now was the time that he did.

'Look, if it's about what happened with us—'

'It's not.'

'No?'

'No.'

There was a beat of silence while he processed that, but then he said, 'Well, I wanted to apologise anyway. I reacted too harshly about the baby. It wasn't entirely...your fault.'

'Entirely,' she repeated, and he felt her gaze on him.

He sighed. 'I felt betrayed, Jess. I told you that.'

'And I told you why I couldn't tell you.'

'Yeah, and I understand that. But—' his grip tightened on the steering wheel '—but I wish you'd told me. Warned me.'

She didn't reply immediately. 'I... I couldn't just tell you. Firstly, I barely knew you. And when I started to get to know you,' she said as he opened his mouth to protest, 'Anja had already asked me not to say anything to you about it. So I didn't.' She cleared her throat. 'But I am sorry for my part in...in hurting you.'

He nodded, but couldn't bring himself to say anything. He appreciated her apology. Her loyalty to his sister. But... Well, he'd wanted Jess's loyalty, too. To him.

And that was the real problem.

'If it makes you feel any better,' she said quietly, 'it wasn't simple for me. I *wanted* to tell you. It felt...wrong not to. But—' she lifted her hands '—I couldn't betray Anja's trust. So I settled on telling you the baby wasn't mine and hoped that it would help you, I don't know, understand.'

Dylan felt some of the pieces that had broken inside him come together again. 'I…appreciate that. Thank you.' He paused. 'And I'm sorry, too. For reacting the way that I did. I shouldn't have…been so blunt. I didn't mean what I said about you not being a part of the family.'

She nodded, and the words were the last they said for another few kilometres.

'It wasn't just about you, you know,' he heard himself say into the silence. 'It was difficult for me to hear it because—' He broke off. Told himself to get it over with. 'When I found out my mother knew my father was an addict before she had us, it felt like a betrayal.'

'When did you find out?' she asked softly.

'A few days before his funeral.' He took a deep breath. 'They'd put all my father's stuff in a box at work after it was clear he wasn't coming back. Gave it to me when I first started. I put it in a storeroom and never looked through it until I got the news that he'd died.' Dylan paused, took another breath. 'When I did, I found meticulous records of his expenses dating back long enough for me to see how he'd paid off the house. How he'd set money aside for the staff, for us. And how he'd used everything else to fund his habit.'

'That must have been hard.'

'What was worse was that it proved my father

had his problem long before we were born. Before my parents had even married. And when I confronted my mom about it—' he lifted a shoulder '—it didn't go well.'

'Oh, Dylan,' she said on an exhale. In those two words Dylan heard everything that Jess wanted to say. That she understood his reaction now. That she was sorry it had happened. It soothed something deep inside him.

'Does Anja...?'

'Yes,' he replied when she trailed off. 'I told her about it a few days ago. Hence this little family trip.'

'Are you okay with that?'

He took a moment to think about her question. About how she'd known to ask it. 'I'm not thrilled. Things were...awkward when I saw my mother at Christmas, and we didn't even end up speaking about it.'

'Maybe things were awkward *because* you didn't speak about it.'

'Maybe,' he murmured.

'So this trip might be exactly what you need to move through it.'

He let the words settle in his mind. Felt the hope of it fight back against the burn of betrayal. Maybe things *would* get better after this trip. Maybe, after finally being honest with one another, they would become a family. A real one, without the weight of betrayal and hurt and resentment hanging over them.

But hearing Jess's opinion spoke to his biggest regret. And now all he could think about was how things could have been sorted out so much sooner if he'd just come home.

Or if he'd never left.

'Things seem to be better between you and Anja now,' she said into the silence.

'Better, but not the same.' He ran a hand over his beard. 'It's going to take some time.'

'Of course it will. But progress is progress.'

'Except—' He stopped himself before he could say what he'd been thinking.

'Except?'

'It's nothing.'

'Oh, so you're going to keep quiet *now*?' she asked dryly, and he felt his lips lift.

'Annoying, isn't it?'

She grunted, and his smile widened into a full grin. And perhaps it was that that had him saying, 'I can't believe she didn't tell me about the baby. About any of her fertility issues.'

'It was...hard for her to talk about.'

'But we're *family*. And we were close before...' He let the words linger. They were another reminder of the mistakes he'd made.

'She thought she was a failure,' Jess said. 'I

don't think she wanted to tell you and have you believe that of her, too.'

'*What?* Why would she feel that way? Why would *I* believe that?'

'Because she wasn't thinking logically. She was only thinking about how she couldn't do the one thing that she was supposed to be able to do as a woman.' Jess shrugged. 'I was there, Dylan. She was so hard on herself.'

The words made pain splinter through him. 'I wish I was here. I wish I could have helped her through it.'

'I know.'

'I shouldn't have left, Jess.'

It ripped from him, the admission.

He was suddenly incredibly grateful that a business crisis had delayed Chet and Anja's departure and they weren't travelling behind him and Jess. Dylan had agreed to go ahead with Jess so that they wouldn't have to tell their mother they would be late. It meant that he could take a few minutes to regroup, to recover from whatever had made him tell Jess the thing he worried about most.

He took the next exit, which led to a pit stop that he only realised was familiar after they stopped next to the small café. They'd stopped there on family trips, he remembered, when they'd taken the short journey to visit his mother's family. He didn't dwell on why the familiarity of it was suddenly comforting, or why he held out his hand when he got out of the car, waiting for Jess to take it.

All he knew was that he felt better when she did. More so when they stopped in front of the little pond next to the café, birds frolicking in the water, making the most of the sunny autumn day.

They stood in silence for a long time while he figured out why he'd stopped. But Jess spoke first.

'Do you know why you left, Dylan?'

'Yes.'

'Why?'

So he told her all the reasons he'd figured out himself over the past weeks. And when he was done she squeezed his hand.

'It's normal to turn away from the things you can't deal with,' Jess said. 'We all do it.'

'Anja didn't. She stayed here and faced it. The memories of it. The grief of it.' He watched as a duck dipped itself under the water and shook it off.

'Anja had Chet, Dylan. She had me. She had a support system. One outside of the family that had caused her pain.' He looked down at her. 'It makes a difference.'

'Why are you being so understanding?'

'Why are you determined to torture yourself like this?'

'I'm not—' He broke off, and shook his head. 'It's not torture. It's the truth. I *abandoned* her. Just like our parents did.'

'You didn't abandon her. You took some time to figure out how you were feeling about your parents. About your childhood that was cut short. Did you do it in the right way?' she asked. 'Maybe not. Maybe you should have told Anja about what you'd found out. Maybe you should have shared how you were struggling with your grief and the anger. But that doesn't mean you abandoned her.'

'But my mother—'

'Was a flawed woman. And your father was a flawed man. So are you. We're all flawed,' she said with a smile. 'We all make mistakes. But we move on from them. We learn from them. And you being back tells me you *have* learnt from it.'

She faced him when he didn't reply, and narrowed her eyes. 'You're not only scared about that though, are you?' And only when she asked did he realise that he wasn't. 'What is it, Dylan?'

'I—' He stopped himself, but only for a moment. It was too late to play coy, and he was so tired of keeping it all to himself. 'Why did his death affect me so much? Why am I so unhappy and angry about it when I only really knew him for fourteen years?' He ran a hand over his head. 'Even *saying* that is generous.'

Her hand fell from his, and then lifted to cup his cheek. 'Maybe it's because you're still stuck in the hope that he could have been different.'

CHAPTER FIFTEEN

'WHICH IS FINE,' Jess told Dylan, dropping her hand. 'There's nothing wrong with wishing you had something you didn't.' It felt as if she was talking to herself. 'But you have to let go of the unrealistic expectations if you want to move on. If you want to move forward.'

'You're right,' he said after a moment.

'Don't sound so surprised.'

His lips lifted, taking some of the torture out of his eyes. 'I'm not. It's just…we have a lot in common, don't we?'

'I wasn't talking about me, Dylan.'

'Maybe not, but, despite what you might think, I've learnt how to read you. Enough,' he said before she could protest, 'that I know you were thinking about yourself, too, just now.' He turned to face her and took a step closer. 'Enough to know that something's wrong with you. Has been since before we even took this trip.'

She wanted to tell him that something *was* wrong. She wanted to share her fears with him just as he'd shared his with her. But it wouldn't help. She knew because when he'd told her that he hadn't meant it when he'd said she wasn't a part of their family she hadn't believed him.

'We should probably get back on the road.'

He stared at her for a few seconds, and then gave her a curt nod. She almost sighed, but was afraid the sound would break whatever control had convinced Dylan that he shouldn't press. They were on the road a few minutes later, and Jess settled on looking out at the rolling hills, interspersed with long stretches of green fields and cattle, that they passed.

It was a pleasant trip, driving along the West Coast. Soon they would take the road that led to the coastal town of Langebaan, home to one of the most popular casinos in the Western Cape. The realisation made her think about Dylan's father, and whether his parents had met here, in this town. Whether it had been the start of his father's addiction.

Jess hoped that what she'd been able to offer Dylan at the pond had given him comfort. That it would be enough to help him work through what he was going through. And that once he had he would be able to turn to Anja when Jess was no longer there.

Because the more she thought about it, the more she realised that she had to leave. If she didn't have a purpose, what use would she be? She only had to look at her parents to know that. She only had to remember that they'd abandoned her long before she'd abandoned them. They'd done it from the moment she was born, no matter how hard she'd tried to prove herself.

Her father had rejected her even though she'd tried to make herself useful in the company. Her mother… Well, her mother had never really paid any attention to her. They'd never let her forget that her presence in their life hadn't been something they'd wanted.

And it turned out that being unwanted, feeling rejected—abandoned—were all pretty close together on the 'make Jess feel crappy' spectrum.

She hated that feeling. And she was still dealing with the remnants of it from her parents. She didn't need it from her friends, too. So she'd do what she'd done with her parents after she'd realised they wouldn't change and welcome her into their team. She would pull away, put distance between them, so that when the day came and she left, they wouldn't be so surprised.

Because *she* would leave, she thought. She would leave them before they left her.

'You've been quiet today,' Anja said from behind her.

Jess forced herself to give her friend an easy

smile—even more so when she saw that Dylan was behind Anja—and went back to looking at the waves of the ocean in the distance.

Mia Nel's cottage was small but it was situated in the perfect position. Just outside the small town of Langebaan, where it was close enough to get whatever she needed within an hour, and far enough that there weren't many tourists around.

The beach was basically her backyard and for that alone, Jess told herself, the trip was worth it.

'It's been a long day,' Jess said as Anja and Dylan settled into the comfortable outdoor chairs on the small outdoor patio.

'It has been, but that's never stopped you from talking before,' Anja teased.

'Maybe it's this baby I'm carrying,' Jess teased back. 'Crazy genes can do that to you.'

'Oh, don't you dare blame my baby for your sullenness!' Anja's eyes twinkled, and then she grew serious. 'Are you sure you're okay though?'

'I'm fine.'

She felt Dylan's gaze on her, but she ignored it and kept her own gaze on the sea in front of her. It was a fair question. Jess knew that she'd been quiet since they'd arrived. She'd been sociable, of course. Had calmly accepted the love Mia had overwhelmed her with the moment they'd met.

But she'd kept herself from becoming too invested in the emotion. Because she knew it wasn't for her. It was for the baby she carried, and she couldn't forget it or avoid it. Ever since Anja had returned, the idea that Jess's time was running out had only grown.

She shook off the weight that settled on her shoulders at the thought of it. It was for the best. *Reject them before they can reject you*, a voice whispered into her mind.

She closed her eyes for a moment before asking Anja, 'So, what are the final accommodation arrangements for the trip?'

It did its job at distracting Anja, and Jess felt the air loosen in her lungs in relief. Though she couldn't deny it was also because she and Dylan would be spending the night in Mia's spare rooms, while Anja and Chet stayed in a cottage they'd rented a few doors down.

She didn't want to be alone with Dylan now. Not with his piercing gaze. Not with the knowing looks.

She felt as if he was looking straight through her. No, it felt as if he was looking straight *into* her. Into the part of her that was cowering like the little girl she'd been when she'd first realised her parents didn't care for her like other parents cared for their children.

It was annoying, being dragged back into the

past. Which was why, as soon as the conversation lulled between the three of them, Jess excused herself for the night. She still had to face her demons, but if she wasn't near Anja and Dylan she wouldn't be tempted to belong.

She hoped.

'She's acting weird, isn't she?' Anja asked Dylan as soon as Jess left for the night.

'Yep.'

'Did she say anything to you on the way over?'

Do words of wisdom about my own emotional problems count?

'No. I asked, but she pretty much gave me the same answer she gave you when you asked.'

'It's so *strange*,' Anja said with a shake of her head. 'Jess isn't like this.' There was a beat of silence before she said, 'Do you know if something happened?'

He debated with himself about whether he should tell Anja. The truth had been working out pretty well for them. His relationship with Anja was slowly improving because of it. And he knew once they had a conversation with their mother they would finally get some closure.

Honesty had brought him a lot of what he'd wanted since he got back. Honesty and Jess. He sighed.

'It could be the fact that we…that I…'

Probably should have figured out what you were going to say before you started talking, dummy.

'It could be because of me.'

'Because of you?' Anja repeated in that slow way she had that told him she was trying to hide her real feelings.

'Yes. While you were gone, Jess and I…' He ran a hand over his head, again unsure of how to describe what had happened between him and Jess over those days before Anja had returned. 'We got close.'

'Got close?'

'Are you going to keep repeating what I say?'

'Yeah, I am. If that's what it takes to keep me from knocking your head against the table.'

And there it was, he thought, and braced for the onslaught.

'Are you telling me, Dylan Theo Nel, that you are *seeing* my best friend? The woman carrying my child?'

'We're not seeing each other. Nothing that official.'

'Nothing…' He thought he saw the colour drain from her face. 'Please don't tell me that "got close"—' she lifted her hands in air quotes '—is a metaphor for some kind of hanky-panky—' She broke off. 'I think I'm going to puke.'

'Oh, stop being so dramatic,' he said, though he'd expected the reaction. 'Nothing happened.' Not in the way she thought, at least. 'But we did have…something.'

'She told me I had nothing to worry about.'

'Because there was nothing to worry about when you asked her. We both knew something between us would be complicated, so neither of us wanted to pursue it.'

Again, not entirely the truth, but only because he was just realising what the truth was as he said it. *He* wanted to pursue it. He had wanted to pursue it from the moment he'd met her. From that first kiss. And still he wanted to. The realisation stumped him.

A long silence passed before Anja spoke again. 'When you say there was nothing to worry about when I asked, does that mean there is now?'

'Depends on whether you're worried about me and Jess being together.' As soon as he said it, he realised how much he wanted Anja to be okay with it. And suddenly the conversation took on a whole new importance. 'Are you?'

'Am I—? Hold on.' Anja lifted a hand. 'I'm trying to process everything you've just said in the last few minutes. It's going to take some time.'

Since he needed some time himself, he didn't

say anything. Instead, he tested how he felt about this latest development.

Of course, he'd known there was something between him and Jess. What he *hadn't* known was how invested he was in that something.

It didn't make sense, he thought. At least not on paper. They'd only known each other for a few weeks. And only two days of that time had been spent on something resembling dating. The rest of the time they'd either been arguing or talking about things so difficult for them that dating had been the last thing on their minds.

But the facts couldn't explain why his heart thudded that much harder when she was around. Why he couldn't keep his eyes from straying to her. Why he wanted to see her reaction to jokes that were made, or stories that were told. Why he still thought about their kisses, and how much he wanted to repeat them.

It didn't explain why he felt so comfortable that he *could* talk to her about things. Or why he sensed that she was unhappy about something. No, the facts couldn't explain any of that. And it was finally occurring to him why that was.

He was falling for his sister's best friend. The woman carrying his niece or nephew. The woman he'd only just met.

And none of the reasons he'd told himself why that was a bad idea seemed to matter any more.

His lips curved.

'Okay, I'm done thinking,' Anja said, and Dylan hid his smile. He didn't want her to think that he was mocking her. 'I'm not going to say that I'm happy about this development. It's messy. And complicated. And, I don't know, it feels incestuous.'

Dylan frowned at what he once again thought was an exaggeration, but kept the opinion to himself.

'But clearly whatever's going on between you and Jess…means something. To both of you.'

'Not sure I'd go that far,' he muttered.

'No,' Anja said immediately. 'Me not totally freaking out about this does not mean I'm going to counsel you on Jess's feelings.' She frowned, and then sighed. 'Except to say that Jess was… hurt by her parents. It takes a long time for her to trust, and if you've done something stupid— which, knowing you, you probably have—it'll take longer for her to get there. But now that you've mentioned it—' she slid a hand through her hair '—I did notice *something* between you. Coming from both sides.'

'Really?' he asked, and was only slightly disgusted by the optimism he heard in his voice.

Anja's face broke into a smile. 'Yes, you dork. Now, back to what I was saying. It's complicated, and it's messy, but…but if it's what you two want, then I'll support it. Just don't, you know, do it, until my baby is out of the way.'

'Firstly, what is wrong with you? And secondly…thanks, An.'

'Don't thank me yet,' she said and stood. 'I'm going to be pretty miserable about this for the foreseeable future.'

'Completely understandable.'

She narrowed her eyes, and then sighed. 'Don't complicate things if it's not worth it, okay?'

'Okay.'

'And don't…don't hurt my friend.'

'I won't.'

Anja left with those words, and Dylan sat back with a smile, watching the waves crash into the boulders and then pull away. It hadn't been the easiest conversation to have but, once again, Dylan felt that his honesty had paid off. Not only because he'd told his sister the truth about things that had happened between him and Jess, but because it had clarified a lot for him.

First, it *was* worth it.

Second, he would do his best not to hurt Jess.

And third, he was going to convince Jess of both those points, no matter how long it took.

CHAPTER SIXTEEN

'So,' JESS SAID the next afternoon, 'I just had a chat with Anja. And it was…surprising, to say the least.'

She and Dylan were at the restaurant where they'd all just had lunch. She'd spent the morning walking through town—if it could be called walking, considering the number of times she'd rested—while Dylan, Anja and Chet had spent the morning with Mia. She hadn't minded entertaining herself. Understood that the reason they were there was so that those conversations could happen.

But that afternoon they'd all had lunch together. Afterwards, Mia had an appointment with a friend, and Anja and Chet had decided to drive to the next town to buy some things for the baby. Which left her and Dylan alone.

Handy, considering she had a bone to pick with him.

'You told her that we kissed?'

'What? No, of course not.'

'Then why did she follow me to the bathroom to tell me that she's okay with us being together?'

'She did that?' His lips twitched, but he shook his head. 'I'm sorry, I didn't realise she would speak to you about it.'

'*It?* What is *it?*'

'I...might have told Anja that there was *something* between us. Not that we'd kissed or anything,' he said quickly. 'But that there was... something.'

She opened her mouth, and then shut it again. Figured it would be better to keep the first words that wanted to come out of her mouth to herself rather than hurl them at him. But the entire exchange had made her feel sick, and she drank from the bottle of water she'd ordered with her meal before she spoke.

'So, let me get this straight. You told my best friend—the mother of the child I'm carrying—that there was *something* between us.'

'Yes.'

'Why?'

'Because there *is* something between us.'

'No, there isn't.' He gave her a look, and she gritted her teeth. 'Maybe there *was*, but we both know that there can't be.'

'Why not?'

'Because…' She trailed off, realising now that her main reason had been Anja, and that no longer seemed to be a problem. 'Because I'm carrying your niece or nephew and you don't agree with that choice,' she finished triumphantly.

'What?' he said, his face twisted. 'That's not true.'

'Isn't it?' she asked mildly. 'Because I distinctly remember your objections to me being a surrogate for someone else.'

'That was before I knew it was Anja's baby.'

'So your concerns aren't valid any more because this baby is your sister's?'

He ran a hand over his head, and she recognised the action as something he did when he was thinking. 'No,' he said finally. 'They still are. But I guess at least I know I'll be there for you now. We all will be. So, you know, you won't have to go through whatever you go through alone.'

It took her a while to figure out how she felt about his words. About the fact that he assumed he would be there for her. That they all would be there for her. It was as if he knew exactly what her biggest fear was, and was speaking directly to it.

It melted her damn heart.

But it couldn't, she told herself. Because it

wasn't real. She wasn't only deluding herself into believing that it was.

'So that made you comfortable enough to tell Anja about us?'

'Well,' he said, leaning forward, 'we both noticed you haven't been yourself the last few days. She asked me about it yesterday and I told her that…it might have been because of me.'

She stared at him, and then she laughed. 'You are *so* full of yourself.'

His eyebrows lifted. 'You're saying I'm wrong?'

'I'm pretty sure I told you that you were in the car on our way here.'

'So I don't have anything to do with the way you've been acting lately? Nothing?' he repeated, as though, somehow, repeating it would change her mind.

It didn't, but it *did* point out that while he wasn't entirely the reason for her pulling away, he was certainly a part of it.

'There's too much going on for me to simplify it like that,' she replied softly. 'And you telling Anja makes it…worse.'

'Why?'

'Because now she has another reason—' She stopped herself from saying the words. From saying that Anja knowing about whatever had happened between her and Dylan would just give her another reason to abandon Jess when it was all over.

She'd been surprised when Anja had spoken to her earlier, and her first thought—her first fear, she knew, remembering how her throat had closed—had been that.

And even though her friend had told her she was fine with it, could Jess believe her? And if she could, how would that work? Would she date Dylan and be forced to see how little she meant to their family day after day?

'Jess,' Dylan said, his expression telling her that he'd been trying to get her attention for some time. 'What's going on with you?'

'Nothing.'

'It's *not* nothing,' he said, and slammed a hand on the table. She resisted a wince, and met his eyes evenly.

'You don't have to believe me. But I'm not going to tell you. No matter how hard you slam your hand against the table.'

'I'm sorry,' he said, but his jaw was still clenched. 'You're just so damn *stubborn*. It's frustrating.'

His brows were knitted together, the anger clear in the planes of his face. And all she could think about was how cute he was when he was angry. She sighed at the flutter in her stomach.

'Don't feel like you have to entertain me for

the afternoon. I wouldn't want to frustrate you more than I already have.'

'Jessica.' It was said on a soft exhale of air, and again she watched Dylan rub a hand over his face. 'I don't know what I'm going to do with you.'

'You don't have to do anything with me.'

'Except that I want to.' His hand fell down to the table. 'Hell if I know why, but I want...you.'

Her heart thudded, and she gripped the napkin that had been beside her hand tightly in her fist. 'Is that why you told Anja? Because you *want* me?'

'I told Anja because I wanted to be honest with her. You encouraged me, remember?' She nodded, unable to speak. 'So I decided to go for it. To put everything on the line. And it's been working. Really well. We've finally made... progress. Real progress. In our relationship, *and* with Mom. So when she asked me, I thought I'd be—' he shrugged '—honest.'

She couldn't argue with his logic. Not when she could see how freeing it had been for him. 'I'm glad it's been working for you. I just wish you'd come to speak with me before you told her. Or, at the very least, warned me that you *had* told her.'

'I am sorry for that. But I meant what I said earlier. I didn't think she'd actually talk to you.'

He shook his head. 'I should have known that she would, though. You're best friends.'

She didn't reply. Not when he made it sound so simple—so *special*—and she didn't know if it was.

'There's somewhere I want to take you.'

'What?'

'You said I didn't have to spend the afternoon with you, but as soon as I found out we'd be alone I knew I wanted to. So you don't have much of a choice.' He grinned at her, and called the waitress to get the bill.

'Are you kidnapping me?'

'Do I have to?' he said wryly, and she couldn't help the curve of her lips.

'It probably wouldn't look good for you, kidnapping a pregnant woman.'

'I could do it,' he said sombrely. 'For the greater good.'

She snorted. 'What greater good? Keeping your afternoon plans?'

'Exactly. Now, are you going to come with me, or do I have to resort to Plan B?'

'And you called *me* frustrating,' she replied, rolling her eyes, and got up with Dylan as soon as he paid the bill.

He chatted as they walked and, since that wasn't the kind of word she'd thought she'd ever associate with Dylan, it made her think that he was nervous. The thought was just as unwelcome as when she'd thought him angry and cute, but this time she didn't push it away.

Instead, she chose to indulge herself.

She was walking along the beach with a handsome man. A man who'd said he *wanted* her. The thrill she'd forced away before went through her spine now, and she relished it. It wouldn't be long before reality set in again. Before she was forced to face it and the fact that Dylan would tire of her eventually. He would figure out that *wanting* was temporary, and needing soon replaced it.

And no one had needed Jess in a long time.

So, for now, she would enjoy it.

Jess looked up when Dylan stopped walking, and for the first time noticed that they'd reached the pier.

'Are we going to be…watching the boats go by?' she asked when the seconds passed and he didn't say anything. It was the only thing she could think of, since there was no one around except a large boat at the edge of the pier and others in the distance.

'No,' he replied. Were those nerves she heard in his voice? 'We're going to watch for whales.'

'Really?' She perked up. 'That's awesome. Can you see them from here?'

'No,' he said again, and now she *definitely*

heard the nerves. 'But we can see them from the boat.'

He nodded in the direction of the boat she'd noticed earlier, and she frowned. 'You mean we're going to...sit on that boat and watch the whales? I guess that would work, but—'

'No, Jess. We're going whale-watching in that boat. With it doing what it's supposed to do. You know, sail.' He lifted a hand, and then dropped it again. 'I hired the boat for the afternoon.'

CHAPTER SEVENTEEN

'YOU HIRED...?' JESS's voice faltered. And then she said, 'You hired a boat for this afternoon. For...a day trip? With a couple of people?'

Her reaction was making his spur-of-the-moment decision seem like a bad one. And he hadn't thought it was. At first. But from the moment they'd left the restaurant, he'd been thinking exactly that. She was *not* dissuading him of that notion.

'No, for the two of us. I wanted you to be comfortable, and I thought that it might give you a break from thinking about...whatever's going on with you.'

He held his breath as she considered his words.

'I have one question for you,' she said after what felt like for ever, turning to him. The wind fluttered through her hair, making the wavy strands of it stir. He felt the movement mirrored in his chest.

'What?'

'Are you going to take your shirt off?'

It took him a moment to realise she was teasing him, and the only reason he did was the saucy grin she gave him that had different parts of his body stirring.

'Only if you plan on watching me,' he said in a growl.

She pretended to think about it. 'Well, there *is* an art to it.' Paused. 'And I *have* become somewhat of an expert on watching you without your shirt on—'

He cut her off with a kiss. Quick and hard. And pulled away before he could be tempted into savouring the taste of her lips—or the surprise on her face. Instead, he took her hand and led her to the boat.

He helped her on board, and then handed her a safety vest before putting on his own. When he was done, he nodded to the captain and they were off.

He'd been teasing her when he'd told her she should watch him. Which was ironic now, considering that he couldn't keep *his* eyes off *her*. She was captivating. She grabbed his arm whenever she saw something—or thought she saw something—her face alight with excitement. And clasped her hands together when that something turned out to be a whale.

They were lucky enough to spot a seal at one point, too, and the absolute glee in her expression made every reservation he'd had about taking her on a boat trip worthwhile.

'I can't believe I've never been on one of these before,' she said as the captain turned the boat around. She accepted the water he'd got from the bar, and drank from it thirstily before continuing. 'It feels like it should be a compulsory experience for everyone at least once in their lifetime.'

'I'm glad you enjoyed it,' he said with a smile, and sat back, enjoying his own drink.

'Oh, don't be so smug. There was very little chance I wouldn't have enjoyed it.'

'There was enough of a chance. What if you got seasick? A high possibility, considering you're pregnant.'

Her hand immediately went to her belly. 'I didn't really suffer from motion sickness before, and I'm happy to say carrying this little guy or girl hasn't changed that.'

'How has it been?' he heard himself ask.

'The pregnancy?' He couldn't pretend he hadn't asked. He nodded. 'Good, for the most part. I was exhausted the first trimester. Still am, though it hasn't been quite as debilitating since.'

'Do you enjoy being pregnant? You don't

have to answer that if you don't want to,' he said quickly when she frowned.

'No, it's not that. I just haven't really thought about it.'

The hand on her belly started to move, and he watched as she drew little circles, over and over, around her stomach. It wasn't the first time he'd seen her do it, but it *was* the first time a small, unknown part of him had stirred.

'It hasn't been a bad experience so far,' she said. 'I know it can be, so I'm one of the lucky ones who doesn't puke at every opportunity. So, I guess physically I don't mind it.'

'You don't mind that your body won't ever be the same again?'

She gave him a look. 'Is that really the question you're going with?'

He felt heat creep onto his face. 'I didn't mean it like that.' And then he wondered what 'like that' meant, and the heat become fiercer. 'I just… I don't know. Forget it.'

She laughed and, mingled with the sound of the water crashing against the boat, it sounded magical. 'Oh, I know what you meant. It was just too good an opportunity to miss.' She tilted her head, and then looked out at the sea. 'It's not that I don't mind it. I just keep thinking that it'll be worth it.'

'Even though it isn't your child?'

She looked at him, and it almost made him regret asking. But she answered him.

'Yes, I think so.' There seemed to be a long time between her answer and the next words she said. 'Anja was...devastated after the miscarriage.' She lifted a hand. Let it drop. 'That doesn't even seem like the right word to use. It's too...neat. Tidy. It doesn't describe how she sobbed every day for two weeks. Her entire body wrenched from it.' He saw her fingers curl, tighten. And couldn't blame her when he looked down and saw his fingers had done the same.

'Giving her the chance to have the child she wanted so badly without going through the fear of that again...' She lifted her shoulders. 'Yeah, I guess it is worth it. Even though it isn't my own.'

'You really love her, don't you?'

'I do.' Her eyes filled and she looked away from him. Even when he took her hand and squeezed.

The rest of the trip was quiet, and Dylan worried that Jess had pulled back into herself again. By the time they reached the pier again, he knew that he was right. But he didn't say anything about it as he helped her off the boat, and said his thanks to the captain.

'We should get back to your mom's place,'

Jess said softly when they reached the edge of the pier.

'Sure,' he said easily. 'I know a shortcut. It cuts across the beach though.'

'I don't mind,' she replied after a second, and shifted, looking down at her shoes longingly.

He smiled. 'Need help?'

She gave him an embarrassed grin. 'Would you mind?'

'Sure.'

He bent down and helped her out of her shoes. While he was there, he took off his own and soon they were walking down the beach.

The sky was a soft orange-yellow colour, an indication of the time of day. It had been a nice day, he thought. One of the few they'd get before winter came in full force. Even now he could feel the chill of the cool autumn air, and looked at Jess, wondering if she was getting cold.

But her face was turned up to the sun, her eyes closed, and his feet stopped. Hell, his entire world stopped. She looked like an angel. The light made her bronze skin glow, highlighted the brown of her hair. For the first time he saw the almost blonde strands in between the dark brown, and the discovery had him reaching out to her, taking her hand before he knew what he was doing.

She opened her eyes and turned to look at

him, and the easy expression on her face turned guarded. 'What? What is it?'

'You're beautiful, Jess.'

Her face went red, and he kept her hand in his, not allowing her to turn from him. She wouldn't push him away this time.

'Don't do this, please.'

'Do what?' he asked her softly, tugging at her hand so that she came closer to him. 'Are you asking me not to tell you how beautiful you are? Because I'm not going to stop doing that, Jess. Not when you're the most beautiful woman I've ever seen.'

'Yes, that,' she said exasperatedly. 'You're making it harder.'

'What are you talking about?' But she only shook her head.

It angered him. And anger had him taking her hand and putting it around his waist. He reached his other hand around her waist, and now she had no choice but to look at him.

'You're driving me crazy, Jess. You have been from the moment we got into that car to come here. You give me cryptic answers to simple questions, and there's *pain* in your eyes, damn it.' He tightened his hold on her, afraid of what letting go might mean. 'Do you know what it does to me, to see you in pain?' He barely waited for the slight shake of her head. 'It *kills* me. I don't know how it happened, but I care about you and I can't seem to escape how much I want it to be the same for you.'

'You don't mean it, Dylan.' Vulnerability crept onto her face, and for the first time he saw more than pain. He saw *fear*.

'How can you tell me I don't mean what I feel?'

'Because you *can't*,' she whispered. 'How can you feel that way about me when my parents, who've known me my entire life, don't?'

He felt her arm drop from his waist, but she didn't move away from him. Because of it, he could see the sheen of tears in her eyes.

Because of it, he could brush them away from her cheeks when they fell.

'It's only a matter of time before you, and Anja, and Chet realise there's something about me that's…that's *unlovable*. You'll realise that I'm no longer useful once this baby is born and I'll have to pick up the pieces of my heart when I'm no longer in your lives.'

Her breath shuddered from her lungs, and she rested her head on his chest. It completely undid him. The simple action. The complicated emotions. He held on to her tightly. As though somehow he could squeeze those insecurities—those absolutely ludicrous insecurities—out of her.

But her words had cleared up a lot for him.

She was afraid the people she loved most in the world would abandon her. And it made sense, too, since the people who were *supposed* to love her most in the world had.

And she was scared about her surrogacy. For once, he thought, she'd had a natural reaction to her unusual situation. And now he knew where *his* hesitation had come from, too. From a fear that she would be hurt. That giving the baby she carried to someone else would damage her in a way she wouldn't be able to recover from.

But *her* fear was much less selfish than that. She was scared Anja wouldn't want her any more. And in that moment Dylan suddenly realised how much Jess loved his family. His thoughts went back to everything she'd said about carrying the baby, about doing it for Anja, and he realised that she already *was* a part of his family. She just hadn't realised it yet.

But, most importantly, her words had made him realise how wrong she was. Because she *was* lovable.

Because *he* loved her.

CHAPTER EIGHTEEN

IT WAS INCREDIBLE, the things Dylan could get her to reveal. She looked up into those eyes that saw everything, into the arresting features of his face, and knew she didn't have a chance against the onslaught of emotions.

If she added how full her heart felt because of the way his arms held her close to him, as though he would never let her go, she was helpless.

And hopelessly in love.

'I'm sorry, I shouldn't—'

'No,' he said, cutting her off. 'You should have. We might not know what we are yet, Jess, but you can tell me anything. And I'll be there to listen.'

A lump sat in her throat. 'You don't—'

'I do, and you're going to stop doubting it.' He pulled back from the embrace, both her hands in his now. 'I know you've been hurt. And abandoned. You shouldn't have been, Jess.

You didn't deserve it.' His eyes were hot, serious, and she almost, almost believed him. 'You didn't deserve it, Jess. I'm saying it again because I need you to hear me. To believe me.'

Was her face that obvious to read? 'I do.'

'No, you don't. And that's fine for now. Because we believe what our experiences teach us, and your experiences haven't shown you that you can believe me.' He paused. 'Or they have, but you haven't seen it.'

'What do you mean?'

'How long have you been friends with Anja?'

'You know the answer to that,' she said softly. 'Two years.'

'Has she done anything in the last two years to make you believe that she wouldn't be there for you once the baby's here?'

She shook her head.

'Then why do you think that she won't be?'

She couldn't answer him when the lump in her throat doubled. It was accompanied by tears burning in her eyes. It took all of a few seconds for them to roll down her cheeks and, for the second time, Dylan brushed them away.

He had a tender look on his face, and she hated what it did to her heart. No, that wasn't true. She didn't hate it at all. But she *was* afraid of it. Because she'd never felt this way before, about anyone, and she didn't know if she could trust him…

'What's it going to take for you to believe me?'

'Kiss me,' she heard herself say. Surprised herself with the words. But then she wanted it more than she'd thought possible. 'I want you to kiss me and make me believe that—'

His lips were on hers before she got a chance to finish her sentence, and she sank into the kiss. Sank into the moment.

For her, the moment was goodbye. It was setting aside the hope he'd stirred in her, and placing the love she'd only just discovered she had for him in a box somewhere inside her, to visit, to cherish whenever she felt strong enough.

But goodbye had never felt so good in her life. It had never come with a strong man holding her in his arms, with his hands caressing her body. It had never caused her spine to tingle, and her breasts to ache. She pressed closer to him, wanting to give him all that she had inside. Wanting to tell him how much he meant to her. Wanting to make sure that one day, when she was no longer there, he'd remember this kiss on the beach.

That he'd remember the passion, the tenderness. That he'd remember how her hands felt on his body, sliding up, underneath his shirt, kneading, skimming. That he'd remember the moan he gave when she scraped her nails lightly over his back, and the one that came from her when he nipped at her lip in response.

They drew away from each other, breath shuddering from their lungs, and then Dylan lifted his hand and set it on her cheek, his gaze intense as it met hers.

'I'm not going anywhere, Jess. And I'm going to prove it to you.' His thumb grazed across her cheek. 'You can believe me.'

'Why?' she asked, her heart hurting. 'Why is it so important that I believe you?'

'Because I love you.'

He stopped her reply with another kiss, and this time she was swept away in it. She didn't think about what he'd just told her, only felt it, and allowed the sweetness of his kiss to convince her to believe it.

And it did.

The time when they kissed, when their tongues tangled with one another in a sweetly intense duel, Jess believed that Dylan loved her. That he wouldn't leave. She could see herself as a part of his world, as a part of his family. She would give birth to Anja's child, and she'd still be a part of their lives.

Her own life wouldn't change all that much. She'd get a new job and find her own place, but she'd still see the people who'd changed her life so much. And there would be a baby she'd share a special bond with, who would enrich her life further.

Fantasy, she thought, but gave herself a few more minutes of it before pulling back.

'Dylan,' she said hoarsely.

'Hmm?' He smiled when he looked at her, but it faded. 'What?'

'We can't—'

'No,' he said, taking a step back. She immediately felt colder, and only then noticed the sun had lowered and it was dusk. 'Don't say that we can't. Say that you don't. Because that would be the only reason why we can't.'

She opened her mouth, tried to say what she needed him to believe. But she couldn't. Because she'd been hurt in her life by rejection, by abandonment, she wouldn't hurt someone else in the same way. Especially when it wasn't true.

'You feel the same way.' The darkness that had been on his face lifted.

'I didn't say that.'

'Because you're scared.'

He saw right through her, she thought, and resented it so very much. 'How far is your mother's place from here?'

'Jess—'

'How far?' she asked tersely.

'A couple hundred metres.'

'So let's get to it.'

She walked in the direction she remembered he'd been leading them in, and sighed in relief when he fell into step beside her silently. She didn't want to talk any more. Not to him, not to Anja. All she wanted was to go home and—

She cut her own thoughts off when she realised she'd thought about Dylan's house when she'd pictured home. That she'd thought about *him*. It had her feet stopping. Had her grabbing his hand, pulling it and forcing him to stop with her.

'I love you, too, Dylan,' she said hoarsely. 'But it doesn't change anything. It can't,' she said when she saw him open his mouth. 'It can't change anything because I'm… I'm not strong enough to deal with whatever might happen if this doesn't work out.'

'It'll work out.'

'You don't know that,' she said, and shook her head. 'No, it's just better for us to…'

Her voice faded as she realised she didn't know what would be better. Or, she thought, what would be worse. For her to fall into this web of hope they'd spun around them, only to find out she'd been fooling herself—she'd been fooling her heart—in the process? Or to ignore it, and constantly be tempted by the hope—the *love*—that Dylan was telling her to believe in?

She had to figure it out, and she couldn't do it with Dylan by her side.

'I'm not going anywhere,' Dylan said softly, and for the briefest moment Jess thought that she'd spoken out loud.

'You say that now.'

'So, I won't say it any more,' he replied simply. 'I'll show you.'

He leaned forward, kissed her forehead, and then continued walking back to his mother's cottage. After a moment Jess followed, her head and her heart a mess.

Since Dylan had never told a woman outside of his family that he loved her, he wasn't quite sure what should happen afterwards. But having her avoid being alone with him… Well, it was safe to say that that hadn't even made his list of possible consequences.

Especially since she'd told him she loved him, too.

And yet, as soon as they reached the cottage that night, Jess excused herself for the evening. And then she made sure that there weren't any more opportunities for them to be alone for the rest of the trip.

It was fairly crafty—it clearly required a lot of manoeuvring—and, if Dylan was honest with himself, she impressed him with her efforts. She woke up before he did, disappeared for a walk on the beach and only returned when everyone had arrived for breakfast. If she woke up later than he did, she would only appear after his mother had already got up and would dive into the breakfast preparations, using it as an excuse not to speak with him.

She went to bed before he did. Stuck to his mother's side at every spare moment. When Anja arrived, she'd switch between the two. And Anja was the perfect deterrent, he thought, remembering how she only needed to send him a look when he tried to get Jess alone and he would abandon his efforts.

If he hadn't understood it—expected it, even, knowing what he did about Jess now—he would have been more offended. But he *did* understand. He understood that she was scared. Terrified, he corrected himself, thinking about her expression on the beach. And the only way she would get over that fear was if he showed her that she had nothing to be scared of.

Which he could focus on now, he thought, since his trip to Langebaan had been somewhat successful.

Their conversations with their mother had been…hard. Hard and painful and, at times, ugly. His mother had greeted him with the nerves, the hesitation he'd come to expect from her. That had always been her personality, though he couldn't deny that there had been a part of him hoping she'd come out of her shell after their father's death.

But it seemed his death hadn't changed that much for his mother. When Anja had asked her why she'd chosen to have them, knowing what their father was, she'd broken down. Had defended him at first and, when he and Anja had refused to accept that, had admitted it had been selfish.

But the more they talked—and it had been strange going between tense, difficult discussions and meals with Jess where everyone pretended nothing was wrong—the more Dylan realised it had been more about *hope* than selfishness. He'd heard it loud and clear in the way his mother had described the joy of feeling them grow, move inside her. Of sharing that with their father.

She'd told them her pregnancies had been the only time he'd been the kind of man she'd always wanted him to be. And Dylan had finally realised that he and Anja had been his mother's hope that he would *stay* that man. That each day after they'd been born she'd hoped for that man to pitch up again. And each day, when that man hadn't—when it became clear he'd left for good—she'd mourned.

She'd broken down in front of them. Had told them how sorry she was for failing them by loving their father. By abandoning them. Hearing the words, the apology, had loosened something inside Dylan. Perhaps because for the first time he believed that she wanted to make up for it. And that maybe she would finally become the woman—the mother—Dylan had always hoped she would be.

It didn't magically allow him to forgive her. And it hadn't done much to change his opinion of his father. But it *had* made him think that things weren't as black and white as he'd thought. Perhaps if he'd still been alive, Dylan could have had the same conversation with his father. Maybe that would have given Dylan a glimpse into the psyche of the man he'd resented all his life. Maybe it would have helped Dylan to understand him.

Now, Dylan realised that his grief was part dealing with his father's abandonment, half wishing that he hadn't died so that Dylan could have tried to understand him sooner. The guilt that came from that—the regret—had merged with his anger and that had made Dylan *grieve*.

He knew it would take him time to work through it all, but Dylan was choosing to move forward. Moving forward meant working on forgiving his parents for not being who he'd wished they had been. For abandoning them. It meant working on accepting who his mother was, and learning to move on from who his father had been. It meant appreciating the closeness he and Anja had started forging again, and making sure that she knew he would never jeopardise their relationship as he had in the past.

And, most of all, moving forward meant making sure Jess knew he was serious about showing her he loved her.

'This must be torture for you,' he said mildly into the silence in the car. Jess might have been able to avoid him in Langebaan, but on their way home it was just the two of them. He almost enjoyed the sound of her shifting in her seat.

'I don't know what you're talking about.'

'Of course you do,' he replied. 'You hate being alone with me.'

'That's not true.'

'Really? Because I clearly recall you honing the skill of avoiding it over the last few days.'

'I did—' She broke off when he gave her a look, and then sighed. 'I don't hate being alone with you. I just know that being alone with you is…tempting.'

He felt his lips curve. *Tempting?*

'Yes, tempting.' His head turned in time to see her roll her eyes. 'You know you are.'

'And I'm not even shirtless,' he said with a smirk, and chuckled when she slapped at his hand on the gear knob. He let the silence that fell on them sit, felt her get restless as it did. He didn't mean for it to make her uncomfortable enough to talk to him, but he couldn't deny he didn't appreciate it when she spoke.

'I don't get it. I don't get *you*.'

'What are you talking about?'

'Why are you…why is this…why don't you sound annoyed with me?'

'Oh, I'm annoyed with you,' he replied easily. 'I'm pretty annoyed, actually.'

'I know I shouldn't have avoided you, but it was easier than—'

'And that's why I'm annoyed,' he interrupted. 'Not because you avoided *me*, but because you're avoiding your feelings for me. That you see them as complicated.'

'And you don't?'

'No.'

'You really don't think our admission of love for one another is going to complicate our lives when we get back?'

His heart did a flip. 'No. Because it won't.'

Seconds passed, and Dylan felt himself grow anxious, the easiness of the silence before gone.

'You know I'm moving out of Anja's place soon, right?' she said finally, and he softly ex-

haled the air he didn't realise he'd been holding in his lungs.

'When?'

'Chet told me he'll be finishing work on my
flat the end of next week.'

'Okay.'

Minutes passed this time. 'And I'm not going
to work for Anja after the baby is born.'

'You're...' His hand tightened on the wheel.
'Does Anja know?'

'Not yet. I'll tell her, though.'

'When?'

'At the right time.'

'I don't think there's going to be a right time
for that conversation,' he muttered.

But she replied seriously, 'Probably not. But
I can't work for her any more. Especially not
after I give birth.'

'Is that your plan, Jess?' he asked quietly.
'You're going to push away the people who
love you?'

'I'm going to *protect* myself.'

'No, you're pushing us away.' Dylan told himself to stay calm. 'I know what it's like to be
abandoned. And I know the fear that it'll happen
again can make you want to abandon the people
you care about before they can abandon you.'
He only then realised how true his words were.

'I'm not abandoning anyone,' she said. 'I'm

trying to make sure this whole process is…easier on all of us.'

He didn't reply immediately. Instead, he took his time thinking about what he wanted to tell her. 'Do you know what this trip made me realise?'

'What?'

'That that fear of abandonment will stay with you until you let the people who love you show you it won't happen.' He let out a shaky breath. 'After my father died, I didn't give my mother a chance to tell me why she'd done what she'd done. And, now that she has, it's helped me to understand and…it'll help me to forgive.'

'Are you telling me to…give my parents a chance?'

'That's entirely up to you. But no. What I meant was that you have to give people chances. You have to give *us* a chance.' He reached over, took her hand. 'We're your family, Jess. Give us a chance to show you that we won't let you down.'

CHAPTER NINETEEN

'BUT YOU'RE NOT my family,' Jess told him with a clenched jaw. 'That's the whole point of this. I'm *not* a part of your family,' she said again, her voice cracking. 'I'm not even a part of my *own* family.'

It still hurt. She *hated* that it still hurt. And that perhaps it always would.

'Then maybe it *would* help to give your parents a chance.'

Surprise had a laugh spilling from her lips. Not because his suggestion was funny, but because it was *ludicrous*. 'I *have* given my parents a chance. I've given them *countless* chances.' She paused. Let the hurt pass through her now. 'They haven't tried to find me in two years, Dylan. They've made what they think about my chances pretty clear.'

'You haven't tried to get in touch with them either,' he reminded her.

'Because I shouldn't have had to. *I'm* the child. I'm *their* child. If they don't care enough about me to find out where I am, why should I care about them?'

'And you're happy with that?'

'I have to be.'

'Jess—'

'Enough, Dylan,' she interrupted. 'Nothing you say is going to convince me that I need to speak with my parents. I know where I stand with them. Even though they haven't heard from me in two years—even though they don't know where I am—they've never tried to find me.'

'You don't know that.'

'I do,' she said, exhausted now. 'And that's the point. I *know* they haven't looked for me. Their only child. I've made it easier for them by leaving. I've made it easier for *myself.* Now I don't have to constantly feel unloved and unwanted. Now I can just move on and—'

'And let *us* love and want you.'

'No.'

'Yes,' he disagreed. 'Look—' he sighed '—maybe I shouldn't have suggested you see your parents. But I just... I just wanted to help take away that pain in your voice.'

'I...appreciate it. But—'

'I'm not done yet,' he interjected. 'You might have had a painful experience with your own family, but you have a new one. A better one. *Our* family.' He reached over and set his hand on hers, where they rested in her lap. 'You're a part of our family, whether you like it or not, Jess. I've had conversations with Anja that have told me you were long before you agreed to carry her child. You are now. And you will be after you give birth, too.'

Tears burned in her eyes and of course there was no way she was able to hold them back. He looked over at her and a few seconds later he pulled the car to the side of the road and drew her into his arms.

She heard her sobs before her mind registered that she was crying. And, once it did, nothing could stop them from wrenching through her. He murmured comfortingly to her, pressed kisses into her hair, and she stayed in his arms as long as she could. Even when the sobs passed, she stayed. And wished she could stay for ever.

But she couldn't, and minutes later she withdrew from his arms. She accepted the tissues he offered her—heaven only knew where'd he got them—and tried to compose herself.

'Sorry,' she said hoarsely.

'Don't apologise.'

'It's pregnancy.'

He smiled. 'Sure.'

'And…well, you know.'

His smile widened. 'I do.'

But, after a few more moments, Jess said,

'Thank you for this.' She waved a hand between them. 'And for all you've said. But—' she inhaled, and then blew out the air shakily '—I'm not ready to…be *in* this. Not until—'

'You're sure I mean what I've said?'

'No,' she said, and then sighed when he shot her a look. 'Okay, maybe. But we both have a lot to deal with when we get back. I have my new place, I need to find a new job, and there's—' she lifted her hands '—the baby. And you just got back after being away for two years. I'm sure you'll have a lot to do at work here, and with your family…'

She faded when she realised it all sounded like excuses. And when she saw the way he was studying her.

She wondered if he could see that her admission of love for him had broken something inside her. That it had healed something, too. That his admission of love had made her want, need, hope for things she hadn't dared give herself permission to want, need or hope for before. That all of it had fear and panic beating inside her in an uncomfortable rhythm and she needed time to deal with it.

'I can give you time, Jess,' Dylan said, and Jess wondered if she'd said aloud what she'd been thinking. Or maybe he could just see through her, like she suspected.

'I can give you all the time you need,' he continued, and something flickered in his eyes that made her heart throb. 'Just…don't push me away. Don't push any of us away. Let us figure it all out. Together.'

Feeling a little helpless, she nodded, and after another few moments Dylan pulled his car back onto the road. For the rest of the trip, Jess couldn't help but think about what had happened over the last few weeks. And each time she did, she wondered one thing:

What if I believe him?

'Do you think Anja will ever get over the fact that I got another job?'

They were at Dylan's house. A fire was crackling in front of them, rain slamming against the windows around them. Daisy was on the carpet in front of the fire, sulking because neither of them had left her enough space to lie on the couch with them.

It was officially winter, and the weather had given them little reprieve. But Jess didn't mind it so much since she'd spent a lot of it in front of a fireplace, doing exactly what she was doing now.

Dylan, Anja and Chet had helped her with her move. Most of her things had been in storage, and it had been fairly easy to move in. But since she was pregnant, headed into her third trimester then, she hadn't been able to do nearly as much as she'd wanted to. So they'd been her hands, and after a few days she was living in her own home.

Since she was still working for Anja, things had gone on the same for them. Most days she'd spent the evening at Dylan's place after he got home from work. He'd cook for her—or them, as Anja and Chet often joined them for dinner—and the evening would end with a cup of hot chocolate in front of the fire.

Then she'd go home, and do it all over again the next day.

It wasn't a routine Jess had thought possible after they'd returned from Langebaan, but somehow she and Dylan had managed to develop a...relationship that had allowed for it.

Even if that relationship did have a lot more sexual and emotional tension than either of them would have liked.

'Speaking from experiencing how long she can hold a grudge, I think it'll probably take some time.' Dylan was stretched out on the couch next to hers, looking incredibly sexy. She wished she hadn't noticed, just as she had countless times in the last three months. And, just as it had countless times in the last three months, a voice in her head warned her that their current relationship wasn't enough for her.

'It's only been a week, Jess,' Dylan continued, interrupting her worrying thoughts. 'And it's definitely going to take more than a week. Though you should probably leverage the baby now as much as you can.'

'I don't understand why she's not upset with you,' Jess grumbled, forcing herself to play along. 'You're the one who convinced me to interview at your company. Hell, you're probably the reason I got the job.'

'That's not true,' he replied. 'I only recommended you to them. I wasn't involved in your hiring.'

'But what did you think was going to happen when you recommended me?' she asked. 'You're the CEO. If they didn't hire me—'

'I'd have fired them all?' he said in a tone that clearly told her he thought the idea was ridiculous.

She smiled. 'Exactly.'

But Jess knew it wasn't true. She'd been hired into a junior position—something that would have been appropriate for someone straight out of university. Which was fair, she thought, considering her experience meant that she *was* basically just out of university.

But none of the people she'd met had given her the indication that they'd been coerced to see her. And based on the professional, kind and fair way she'd been treated, she didn't think her interviewers believed hiring her would influence the way their CEO treated them.

So while she knew Dylan's recommendation held weight, she liked to think her organisational knowledge and the financial experience she'd gained assisting Anja with the new studio had been the push she'd needed to get the job. Though the fact that they'd agreed for her to start after she'd given birth was *definitely* Dylan.

'Well, it doesn't really matter now anyway since you've already accepted and signed the contract,' he told her. 'And as for Anja not being upset with me... I actually think she prefers you working in the company. It means she knows you'll be taken care of.'

'But she's still mad at me,' Jess complained, and tried to push herself up. When that failed, she tried to get comfortable with the pillow behind her. It was really a bit pathetic, but she couldn't do much since she'd ballooned in her final trimester. Now, even the simplest things were hard.

'Here, let me help.'

She wanted to protest, but she couldn't because, damn it, she needed his help. She tried to hold her breath against his manly scent, against the way it always made her body feel achy and needy. But just like her body had ballooned in the last three months, so had her feelings for him. And while she still wasn't ready to face what that meant, it had heightened her physical attraction to him to the point where she couldn't deny that she wanted more.

'Thanks,' she said when he was done, and leaned back against the pillows again. She'd hoped changing position would help with the strange feeling she had in her back, and for a brief moment she thought that it had. But as soon as she was comfortable again, it reappeared. Almost like a band stretching across the breadth of her back, tightening. It was a little painful.

'I should definitely leverage it,' she said with a huff. 'Being this pregnant is *not* fun.'

He smirked. 'I can't imagine it is. But at least you carry it well.' He sat back down, and she laughed when she saw that Daisy had claimed part of the couch after Dylan had got up.

'You have to say that,' she said once she'd sobered. 'You l—' She cut herself off with a frown. Was she really just going to say because he *loved* her? That went against all the rules she'd given herself about speaking about their feelings for one another. 'Because you love the little thing making me so uncomfortable,' she said instead.

'Well, he or she is family,' Dylan replied with a thin smile.

She knew that smile. It was the one he'd give her whenever he restrained himself from speaking about his feelings for her. He'd agreed to give her time, she thought, but he hadn't agreed to keep himself from talking about how he felt about her. She knew that the only reason he did was because he wanted her to feel comfortable.

And didn't that just make resisting him so much harder?

The band tightened around her back again, and she closed her eyes. Hissed out a breath.

'Hey, are you okay?'

When she opened her eyes again, Dylan was at her side, concern etched into every angle of his face. 'Yeah, I'm okay.'

She gestured for him to help her sit up straight and when he did she took a few moments to breathe.

'Jess, I think we should go to the hospital.'

'No,' she said immediately. 'It's just some… discomfort.'

'No, it's more than that.'

'Braxton-Hicks contractions then. I've been having them all day.'

'All day?' Dylan said with alarm. 'We've been together since this morning. Why didn't you say anything?'

'Because I'm *fine*.'

As she said it, Jess felt something shift and

soon after warmth puddled between her legs. She sucked in her breath. 'Dylan.'

'Yeah?'

'Please tell me that you dropped some kind of liquid on me.'

'No, wh—?'

He broke off when he looked down and saw her stained pants. Jess would have felt embarrassed by it if her heart hadn't started pounding, nearly cutting off her breath.

'Jess, honey, I think your water just broke.'

'No,' she breathed. 'No, it's too early. I think you just spilled something on me.'

'I don't have anything in my hands.'

She hated how gentle his voice sounded. 'Then I peed myself,' she snapped. 'It's three weeks too early for my water to break.'

'So let's get you to the hospital and sort it all out. They can tell you whether you peed once you're there.'

'No.' Now she was pleading. And ignoring how strange it was that they were talking about *pee*. 'Dylan, please, it's not time.'

'You're worried.' It wasn't a question. He brushed the hair from her face and left his hand on her cheek. 'There's nothing to be worried about.'

'Not worried,' she rasped. 'Scared. Terrified. I don't know... I don't know if I can do this.'

'I know. I know you're scared. But you're strong. And you *can* do this. I haven't had more faith in anything than that.' He leaned forward and kissed her forehead.

And in that moment, as ill-timed as it was, Jess could no longer deny that she wanted to be with him. She loved him. And he loved *her*.

'Stay with me,' she told him as the band tightened around her back again. 'Please.'

'I will.'

And he did.

Dylan didn't know he could be so tired. And *he* hadn't been the one to give birth!

He imagined that Jess was feeling a million times worse than he was, except that she was still awake, smiling faintly at Anja and Chet as they cooed at their newborn son.

A nephew, he thought, a grin curving his lips. There was a little boy in his family. Sure, right now he looked all rumpled and new, but one day he would be kicking ball with his uncle who lived right next door. He'd be going on hikes, doing outdoor sports. Dylan figured his imagination would have conjured up much of the same images had his sister had a daughter but, either way, thinking about it was pretty great.

And made all of the turmoil of the last few months worth it.

His eyes settled on Jess again, and he felt his heart swell. She was amazing. It wasn't the first time he'd thought it, and he knew it wouldn't be the last. But witnessing her today...

She'd been amazing.

As soon as they'd got to the hospital she'd turned into the quintessential woman, prepared to do exactly what nature intended of her. She'd screamed in pain—and internally he'd screamed, too, since she'd insisted on holding his hand throughout the process—but as soon as the contraction was over she would go quiet, and softly apologise for acting exactly as anyone else in her position would have.

Six hours later—*six*—Jessie Dylan White had been born. Named after his godparents, Dylan had been told, and he'd had to pretend to drink water when he'd heard to keep them from seeing how emotional he'd felt. Jessie was a good size, good weight and perfectly healthy. And he'd been welcomed into a family who loved him.

He was a lucky kid, Dylan thought. He had great parents, a grandmother who would do her best not to repeat the mistakes of the past, an uncle who was already willing to give him anything he wanted, and a godmother who was a warrior.

He'd seen Jess's face when Anja had told her the name of their son. Had seen the annoyance

Anja had felt for Jess fade away after they'd embraced. He'd known that the annoyance was temporary, and only because Anja had yet to see how important it was for Jess to believe that she was loved not because she'd provided something but just because she was worth it.

He'd spent the last three months proving exactly that to Jess. He'd told her he'd give her time and he had, even when it had pained him to do so. But he'd run from pain before. He'd run from the people he loved. He wouldn't now. Because Jess needed to believe that he'd always be there for her.

So he had been. And it was worth all the anguish when he could see on Jess's face that she finally believed it.

Jess turned her head and met his eyes, and her lips curved into a soft smile. His heart galloped in his chest and he smiled back at her, wondering at how much she'd changed him. Before he'd met her, he never would have enjoyed feeling his heart pound for someone.

Now, he relished it.

The nurse came in then, ushering them out by telling them that Jess needed her rest. He stood when Anja set the sleeping Jessie back into his crib, smiled when she kissed his forehead and moved to follow them out of the room.

'Dylan,' Jess said before he could leave.

'Yeah?'

'You showed up for me.' Tears shone in her eyes. 'I... I believe you.'

'What do you believe?'

'That you love me,' she said with a smile. 'That you'll stay.'

His heart filled. 'I do. I will.'

'You made me believe you.'

'I know.'

'And you waited until I was ready to tell you I believed you.'

'I did.'

'I love you.'

It took him a moment before he could speak. 'I love you, too.'

'And this time I believe that it *will* change everything. Because I believe in you. And I'm going to—' she took a breath, blew it out '—I'm going to wade through the deep, dark waters of commitment for you.' She gave a small laugh. 'I'm really high on pain meds. Can you tell?'

He chuckled, and met the nurse's eye. 'May I?' he asked. With a wink, she gave him a nod and walked out.

And in two short steps Dylan was next to the woman he loved, pressing his lips to hers.

EPILOGUE

'IT'S BEEN TOO long since we've been here,' Jess said, stretching out on the reclined beach chair on what had once been Dylan's mother's back porch. 'Too long, I think.'

'Well, we've had a lot on our plates,' Dylan replied, scooping her into his arms and plopping her down on the day bed just next to where she'd been stretching out before.

She cuddled back against him when he joined her, before realising that she should have been offended by his ungentlemanly behaviour. But by then she was already enjoying where she was too much. In the sun at a beach cottage with the most handsome man she'd ever met.

Who *just happened* to be her husband.

'I guess, but it just seems like a waste. Like we missed opportunities to use this place as a holiday home.'

'We've had plenty of other, just as enjoyable, holidays,' he said, nuzzling her neck. Gooseflesh shot out on her body as it always did when he did that, and she smiled lazily.

'*Very* enjoyable.'

'I like your dirty mind, Mrs Nel.'

'It's something of a talent, I think.'

She smiled and settled back into Dylan's arms, thinking about how much had happened since they'd last been in Langebaan. It had been three years. *Three years.* At first, there hadn't been a reason to return. Dylan's mother had moved to Cape Town once Jessie had been born, wanting to be closer to her family. Wanting to show them that she was different now. And, since Dylan owned the cottage, he'd had it renovated into a larger home since he'd believed their family would expand in the coming years.

He'd wanted it to be a holiday home for them. A place they could come to for some R&R. The renovations had taken a year to complete, and then they'd had their wedding and a brief working stint in Dubai and it had never been a good time to return.

Until now, she thought. She couldn't have planned it any better.

'Dylan?'

'Hmm?'

'I think we should go see my parents.'

Dylan shifted against her and when she looked at him she saw concern in his eyes. 'Why?'

'Well, it's been five years and... I don't know.' She sighed. 'I keep thinking back to what you told me after we left this place three years ago. But I wasn't ready to see them then. I didn't have anything, and I was afraid—' she turned onto her back, let her fingers flutter up to play with his hair '—I was afraid that going back would break me because I had nothing. But now...' She smiled at him, pushed up for a kiss. 'Now, I have everything. And it seems like the right time.'

Jess didn't want to carry around the weight of the negativity she felt towards her parents any more. They were always in her thoughts, the hurt she'd once feared always lurking in the recesses of her mind. She wasn't the same person she'd been when she'd left them—that hurt no longer had the same power over her—and that alone gave her the courage to speak with them. To finally get some closure, and accept whichever form it came in.

Good or bad.

And though she didn't think that they deserved the chance—especially after they hadn't responded to the wedding invitation she'd sent them—Jess now knew that *she* deserved it. She deserved to know whether they regretted their decisions. She deserved to leave them behind if they didn't.

She had a family now, and she wasn't so completely desperate for their love any more. She could move on if she had to. She *had* moved on. But she wanted the opportunity to tell them that she was happily married, successful in her career, and that…

'I'm also pregnant,' she said in a rush, 'and it feels like it's a good time to move on from the past and clear up all the what-ifs.'

She held her breath as she watched the stunned expression on his face.

'You're *pregnant*?'

'Yeah. And it's our baby,' she joked. It was a lame joke, she knew, but she was desperate to break the tension that had suddenly fallen between them.

'I've only known for a few days, and I know we haven't thought about it in some time, so I didn't want to tell you immediately, and we were coming here, and I thought that it would be the perfect time to tell you.' She paused, but he still didn't speak, so she continued, 'I guess I shouldn't have just blurted it out. I should have done something cute and filmed it and put it online.'

She barely paused to take a breath. 'And I shouldn't have sprung it on you after telling you I wanted to see my parents. But I was thinking about our child, and how we'd feel if some day they didn't speak to us. Of course, it's not the same, but—'

He cut her off with a kiss, deep and filled with so much passion and emotion that she felt raw. When he pulled back, he leaned his forehead against hers.

'You're pregnant.'

'Yeah,' she replied, her breath ragged.

'I… I'm going to be a father.'

'Yes.'

'We're pregnant,' he said again, and this time he laughed and gave her another kiss. And when he sobered he said, 'I have no idea how to be a father.'

'I have no idea how to be a mother. But we've figured out a lot together, my love. I think it's going to be okay.'

'Me, too,' he said with a smile.

'So…you're not mad?'

'Why would I be mad?'

'Because…we haven't spoken about it.'

'Recently,' he added. 'But we spoke about it after Jessie was born. And again, after we got married. Life's been so busy since then…' He shook his head. 'I don't know how to be a father, Jess. And heaven knows I had the worst example in the world. But I'll be there for this baby. Our baby.'

He set a hand on her abdomen, and the heat

of it—the sweetness of it—seared through her body. His eyes met hers and what she saw there made her heart fill. 'Our baby, Jess. Yours and mine. We'll figure it out together. And if you need to talk to your parents to help you figure it out, we can.'

She smiled at him. 'I never thought this day would come for me. Where I'm a part of a family that's not broken, about to have my own child. You made that possible for me.'

'I could tell you the exact same thing.'

'Yeah, you could.'

He chuckled and pressed his lips against hers. This time neither of them pulled away.

* * * * *

*If you enjoyed this story,
check out these other great reads
from Therese Beharrie*

*FALLING FOR HIS CONVENIENT QUEEN
UNITED BY THEIR ROYAL BABY
THE MILLIONAIRE'S REDEMPTION
A MARRIAGE WORTH SAVING*

All available now!